HEROICS

Alex Kost

Dedication

This book is dedicated to my family: Mom and Dad; Gram and Pop-Pop; Aunt Lynn and Uncle Kevin; and Kylie and Ryan, the best "siblings" an only child could ever ask for.

Acknowledgments

Heroics would never have gotten past being a simple NaNoWriMo victory if not for the support and editing by select members of the Wiz Crew and a certain fellow Sterling High alumna (you know who you are). Others who shall not be named include two of my English teachers- one middle school, one high school -who made more of an impact on my writing than I think either of them will ever realize.

Dramatis Personae

Heroics

AJ Hamil: 31; black hair; brown eyes; team medic; Caucasian

Casey Cabot: 34; auburn hair; blue eyes; tech coordinator; Caucasian

Jay West: 15; black hair; brown eyes; "Clash"; enhanced speed/endurance; Hispanic

Julian Grey: 17; black hair; brown eyes; "Ghost"; telekinesis; African American

Justin Oliver: 15; dark blond hair; brown eyes; "Archer"; enhanced accuracy; Caucasian

Kara Hall: 13; blonde hair; hazel eyes; "Pilot"; flight/enhanced strength; Native American/Caucasian

Katherine "Kate" Oliver: 16; light brown hair; green eyes; team leader; "Targeter"; enhanced accuracy; Caucasian

Lori Marquez: 14; brown hair; brown eyes; "Torrent"; water manipulation; Chinese

Ray Sampson: 14; black hair; blue eyes; "Blackout"; electricity manipulation; Middle Eastern

Stephanie Cabot: 61; brown hair; gray-blue eyes; boss; Caucasian

Tess "Cass" Cassidy: 30; red hair; gray eyes; mission control; Caucasian

Shade Security

Alice Cage: 55; light brown hair; gray eyes; president; Caucasian

Alison Cage: 19; light brown hair; gray eyes; light manipulation; Caucasian

Wechsler Industries
Gabriel Garrison: 50; graying black hair; blue eyes; head of security; Hispanic/Caucasian
John Wechsler: 55; red hair; gray eyes; president; Caucasian

Other Allies
Alix Tolvaj: unknown; "Thief"; shadow manipulation
Niall Sullivan: 17; black hair; blue eyes; Kate's boyfriend; Caucasian
Ryder Jefferson: 34; black hair; blue eyes; "Jetstream"; tornado creation; Hispanic
Zachary "Zach" Carter: 33; blond hair; hazel eyes; "Kov"; metal manipulation; Caucasian

1

The sound of Central City Bank's less-than-silent alarm pierced through the quiet darkness of 2 AM Caotico City. Lee Francis fumbled out the back door, bags of money clenched in his hands and a ski mask pulled over his face. He glanced around quickly before he bolted down the alleyway towards the road.

Two arrows- one purple, one green -pierced the ground in front of him, forming a perfect X. He skidded to a stop and looked up. On the roof of the building to his right was a teenage girl with brown hair pulled visibly back into a ponytail. She was wearing a purple vest over a white T-shirt, purple gloves, white combat pants, purple boots, and dark purple sunglasses. A purple bow was tight in her grip, and a white quiver was strapped to her back. On the opposite roof was a teenage boy- younger than the girl, but not by much -with dark blond hair; he was wearing the same outfit as the girl, but his colors were green and gray.

"A ski mask? Really, dude? Those are seriously outdated," the boy shouted down.

"And who are you two supposed to be? Archery Boy and his trusty sidekick, Arrow Girl?"

"Wow, and here I thought criminals were friendlier," the girl said sarcastically. "Buddy, it's two in the morning. Can you at least make this a bit more exciting?"

"How's this for exciting?" Francis snarled, pulling a handgun out from his belt. He aimed it at the green-clad boy, but it was stolen by a red blur.

Another teenage boy, this one with black hair, appeared in front of him, grinning. His outfit was similarly identical to the others', minus the weaponry, and his colors were red and black. He looked up at the first boy. "I think I just saved your skin, Archer. Do I get points for that?"

"There's no way he was going to hit me at this distance with a handgun. Besides, there are only points for being the one who takes out the bad guy," the blond boy, Archer, replied. He drew back an arrow, aiming it at Francis. "Which I'm about to do."

"Don't kill him," the girl said, sounding bored. "That would be an awful lot of paperwork, and bad press."

"If you're trying to intimidate me, it's not working," Francis said gruffly.

"What, you're a big, *tough* burglar in a lame mask?" Archer asked mockingly.

Francis laughed. "You kiddos don't know what you're dealing with." He placed his hands before his body and blasted gale-force winds in their direction. The attack seemed to take all three teenagers by surprise, throwing them back. Francis smirked. "Catch me now, kiddos," he muttered as he turned and ran.

Kate "Targeter" Oliver cursed under her breath as the blast of air smacked into her body, throwing her backwards across the rooftop. She tightened her grip on her bow and managed to hold on to it as she smashed into the ground. As she stood again, she touched the white band on her wrist. "Control, our bank burglar just pulled out superpowers," she said to the communications system built into her glasses.

Tess Cassidy, Mission Control, gave a dry laugh through the speaker in Kate's ear. "How many is that this week?"

"This would be number five."

"I think they're magnetically attracted to you, Targeter."

"Maybe they're attracted to sarcasm," Kate retorted.

"Then we're all doomed."

Kate smiled slightly. Tess- who preferred to be called Cass -was herself a former villain. She had gone from being willing to kill Kate and the rest of the team of heroes she now worked with, to being one of the four supervisors who directed them. She was, at times, emotionally distant, but had retained a healthily sarcastic (and sardonic) sense of humor that practically forced Kate to like her. "Can I get some backup, Control?"

"Oh, of course. Why didn't you say so?"

"It's already on its way, isn't it?"

"I dispatched the rest of the team as soon as you told me that our guy has powers. Where was he last headed?"

"Down Bristol Street."

"I'll send them to cut him off. Anything I should warn them about?"

"Nah. He seems to have air-based powers, but I doubt any of the others will have too much trouble with that."

"Okay. They'll meet you at the bad guy."

"Thanks, Control."

"Never a problem."

"Targeter out." Kate leaned over the edge of the rooftop. "Archer, Clash, are you both okay?"

"Yeah, yeah, I'm fine," Kate's younger brother, Justin "Archer" Oliver, replied as he shot a green arrow towards the ground and used the attached rope to slide down to street level.

"It'll take a bigger breeze than that to do much more than irritate me," said Jay "Clash" West as he zipped to Justin's side.

Kate nodded. "Good. The others are going to head off our airhead. You should try to meet up with them and corner this guy before he starts spending his 'hard-earned' cash."

"Yes, Oh Great Leader," Justin said, giving her a mock bow. Smirking, he ran off after Francis.

Jay rolled his eyes. "I don't know why you haven't shot your brother yet, Targeter."

"I often wonder the same thing myself," Kate sighed as Jay bolted away.

Kate ran across the rooftops until she found her two companions again, surrounding Francis along with Julian "Ghost" Grey, Lori "Torrent" Marquez, Ray "Blackout" Sampson, and Kara "Pilot" Hall. The burglar looked furious.

"What's with you guys?" he was yelling. "Don't you have more important criminals to be rounding up?"

"Maybe, but we like taking the stupid ones out first," Justin replied. "Seriously, who robs a bank at night? It's like you're going against all the rules of crime."

"Well *usually* there are fewer people around to give me problems," Francis spat in retort. "Don't make me hurt you! Just leave me alone!"

"You really *are* stupid if you think you can just tell us to walk away and we will. For once I think I agree with you, Archer," Kara said.

"Thanks for the support, Pilot."

Francis, apparently not as amused as Justin, shot a blast of air at her. It caught her in the chest and lifted her up into the air, but she just stayed where she was, floating a foot off of the ground.

"Hello? Pilot? Flight? Good god, it's amazing you can even use those powers." Justin sighed and raised his bow. "Care to do the honors, Ghost?"

"Of course!" Julian replied brightly.

Justin shot a roped arrow just to the right of Francis. Julian held up a hand, and the rope veered off to the side, tying Francis up tightly.

"And here I thought empowered villains were supposed to be difficult," Justin said as Francis fell over.

"Who *are* you people?" Francis demanded.

Kate jumped down and landed in front of him. She smiled as she retrieved her brother's arrow from the tangle of rope around Francis. She then rested her bow on her shoulder and said, "I'm Targeter. These are Archer, Clash, Ghost, Torrent, Blackout, and Pilot." She crouched down so that she could look him in the eye. "You can call us Heroics."

2

Kate walked down the narrow road that snaked through the forest behind the mansion she and the others lived in. The seven teenagers who made up the Heroics team were all orphaned children of superheroes, so they had lived together in the Phantom Mansion for years. The mansion itself was in Fuego Village, a section of mansions, labs, and warehouses just outside of Caotico City. The building, owned by successful scientist and billionaire Stephanie Cabot, appeared from the outside to be a rundown old place; it was surrounded by high walls that hid most of the structure from view, making it easier to pretend that no one lived there. The mansion served as both their home and base and had several secret entrances to keep up the illusion that it was abandoned. Generators, a private well, and a system of Internet and television signals built by Stephanie's daughter Casey kept the inside of the mansion up to date without putting it on the government's map.

As soon as Kate ducked under a low-hanging branch, she found herself in front of a section of the huge brick wall, about six feet from one of the wall's corners. Kate touched the one slightly off-color brick and lifted up the panel that hid the access to the security system behind it. She typed in her security password, clearly said, "Targeter," and then took a step back. A small section of the ground slid away, revealing a dimly lit staircase that led under the wall; Kate descended. The ground slid back shut behind her as she headed down the hallway and, after sixty feet, the hall ended in a thick white metal door. Kate grabbed the handle, pulled it open, and stepped into the base of the Heroics team.

Immediately to her right was the huge training room. Through thick glass walls she could see Julian levitating several items of various weight, while Jay ran on a hamster-wheel-like device, the only thing that could handle his speeds. In front of Kate, Casey was hunched over something in her lab beside the training room, her dark auburn hair pulled back into a bun. Beside the lab was the armory, then the locker room, and then the garage. The control room was tucked away on Kate's left. In the center of the base, across from a small staircase, was a large silver elevator. Kate headed for it, hitting the button for the first floor as she stepped inside.

Justin looked up as Kate joined the team in the first floor's conference room. "Where have you been?" he asked.

"School. I go there, remember?"

"Yeah. No idea why."

"So that I don't end up an idiot like you?"

"Cute."

"You should try going sometime. It'd be good for you."

"I don't see why I should have to-"

"Behave, children," AJ Hamil said as he entered the room.

"AJ, can you make Justin go to school?"

AJ laughed. "I could try, but I'd end up getting shot at."

"Smart man," Justin said, grinning.

AJ Hamil served as the team medic, another one of the adults involved in Heroics and the only one actually qualified to patch them up when they (inevitably) ended up injured. He and Casey had grown up together, and acted like siblings because of it.

As he sat down, the man asked, "Kate, you said that you had something you wanted to talk about?"

Kate sat and nodded. "Yeah, but we should wait for everyone else to get here."

"Casey's getting Julian and Jay now," Cass said as she joined them and took a seat next to AJ.

"Good," Kate said. "Because something's not right."

Casey and the two boys soon joined the table. When they were all gathered together like this, it always struck Kate as amusing that the various races of the Heroics team made them look like they had been cast as some sort of token team on a TV show. The adults were all white, with AJ being a darker-skinned Italian and both Cass and Casey looking paler and more English, but the kids had variety: Ray was the beige-skinned Middle Eastern, Julian an African American with dark brown skin, Jay the olive-skinned Hispanic, Kara the pale-bronze mix of Native American and Caucasian, Lori the fair-skinned Chinese, and both Kate and Justin fair-skinned Caucasians. The fact that, aside from Kara's biracial heritage, each kid was a different race honestly unnerved Kate.

16

Something about the neatness of it all made her feel like she had missed a very important memo when she had first ended up in Heroics as an infant.

Shaking the feeling off, Kate leaned forward. "Does anyone besides me think that it's weird that so many criminals are showing up with powers?"

Justin shrugged. "Maybe they heard that there were superhero teams working in Caotico and came here to challenge us."

"What criminal concerned mostly with making money would *seek out* a tougher area to work? That's just counterintuitive," Julian pointed out.

"Did the crook from this morning say anything about his powers?" Cass asked Kate.

Kate shook her head. "I asked him about how he'd ended up with powers, but he just told me he was going to break out of jail and destroy us all or some other nonsensical villain jargon."

Lori scoffed. "Good luck breaking out of Caotico City Prison. That thing's built to keep in everyone, even empowered people."

"Do you think that the criminals are just suddenly gaining powers?" Jay asked.

"How?" Ray was frowning. "Could it be possible that someone's *giving* them powers?"

"I don't see how," AJ replied. "I mean, it's possible I suppose, but I can't think of a reason why anyone would want to. These aren't exactly the kind of criminals that would be useful to a crime organization or anything."

Kara frowned at Cass, who had an odd look on her face. "What's wrong, Cass?"

Cass shook her head. "Nothing. I'm fine." She started to say something else, but was interrupted when the silver band around her right wrist began to beep and glow red. "Silent alarm went off," she said, getting to her feet.

"Suit up," Kate ordered to her team as she ran for the door.

Bank robbery was apparently the crime of the day. Jay, Kara, and Lori went to the alarm that had interrupted their meeting, while Julian and Ray headed off to an alarm that sounded not long after. Justin and Kate were forced to break away from the group by the time that they got to the city, heading for a third alarm on the outskirts.

"This is stupid," Justin muttered.

"You really are in a *fantastic* mood today, aren't you?"

"I was up at two in the morning, getting stuff thrown at me. So yes, yes I am."

Kate rolled her eyes and rounded the corner onto the street where the latest alarm had come from. She back up immediately, stopping herself from running into a huge man sprinting up the road. He glared down at her. "If I were you, little girl, I'd move."

Kate sighed. "If I could, I would, but I can't, so I won't."

The man swung a bag with some bank's name on it at Kate's head; she ducked out of the way easily. "Wow, way to flat-out tell us that you're the bad guy we're here for." He swung at her again, forcing her to move back once more.

"Mind if I give this a quick ending, Targeter?" Justin asked, pulling his bow off of his back.

"Be my guest."

The man turned on Justin. "What have you got, boy?"

Justin buried an electrified arrow into the man's chest. "That."

The man calmly pulled the arrow out. "The crook world calls me Tank. Do you know why?"

Justin scoffed. "No, but I'm sure you'll tell us."

"I'm invincible! You can't hurt me! You can't stop me! Instead I'm going to take you both down!"

"Aw, man. This is always the annoying part." Kate took a step towards Tank, shooting another sparking arrow at him. It might as well have bounced off of him, for all the damage it did.

Tank grabbed Kate's ankle, completely ignoring her arrow, and threw her into Justin. Both teens flew backwards, slamming into the ground in a heap.

"That went well," Kate said breathlessly.

"I thought we were supposed to be good at this..."

"Yeah, well, tell him that."

Justin fired an arrow at Tank from where he was laying on the ground. "I really hate having the useless power. I mean, ridiculously good accuracy is cool and all, but it's really not going to help us if nothing we hit him with does a damn thing."

"I noticed," Kate muttered, sending another arrow on.

Tank headed towards them, his fists raised. "You should've run when I told you to!"

"Causing trouble, Tank?" a female voice called from behind.

At the sound of her voice, Tank turned and stepped slightly sideways, allowing Justin and Kate to see a figure standing a few feet away. She was wearing black boots, black combat pants, a dark blue t-shirt, a dark blue cloak with its hood raised, and dark blue gloves. Strangely, no part of her face was visible; all identifying features were hidden in shadows.

"Who the hell are you?" Tank demanded. "You aren't dressed like these idiots, so I know you aren't with them."

"I'm not with them, but I am here for them," the girl replied. "And I need them alive, if it's not too much trouble, so why don't you get out of here before you get hurt as well?"

Tank laughed. "You think you could take me down, mystery girl? You won't have any more luck than these two."

The girl echoed his laugh mockingly. "I think you might be wrong about that."

Tank, looking irritated, charged towards the girl but before he got near her, he disappeared into a black hole that had appeared out of nowhere in the ground. The hole then briefly disappeared before reappearing, floating a good fifty feet in the air. Tank fell through it and slammed into the ground.

"What the hell was that?" he demanded as he slowly got back onto his feet.

"I'm a darkness manipulator, Tank: I control shadows. I can move through them; I can move

20

others through them." A thick rope of darkness tripped Tank up so that he fell again, then snaked around him until he couldn't move. "And I can use them. I can use them quite well, actually."

With Tank incapacitated on the ground, the girl turned away. "Hey, wait a minute!" Kate yelled. "Who are you? You can't just-"

"You'll see me again soon, Targeter." A doorway of darkness appeared on the wall next to her. "You'll see me again real soon." The mystery girl stepped sideways and vanished, leaving Kate, Justin, and the furious Tank alone in the street.

In one of the tall office buildings that lined the border between industrial Fuego Village and suburban Caotico City, John Wechsler sat in a chair behind his desk and stared out the large window of the 30th floor. There was a sharp knock on the door, after which a woman with light brown hair and strange, metallic-gray eyes walked into the room. She, like Wechsler, was in her mid fifties, but there was a bright energy in her eyes that made her seem much younger.

"What's the status, Alice?" Wechsler asked quietly, not bothering to turn to face her.

"Tank and Gust are both down. Juke and Wasp are still out there, but they're losing ground quickly."

Wechsler scoffed. "Not very good choices for your little experiment, now *were* they?"

"You know as well as I do why they were chosen."

"That I do."

"And why is it *my* experiment whenever something goes wrong, but *your* experiment when something goes right?" Alice asked bitterly.

Wechsler turned around, smiling. "Now, Alice, don't get worked up. We still have plenty of pawns out there."

There was a quick flash of light, and a teenage girl with light brown hair appeared next to Alice.

"Speaking of which…" Wechsler mumbled.

Ignoring him, Alice looked at the girl. "What do you want, Alison?"

"Juke and Wasp are down. Shall I activate the others?"

"No. But do go find a few more for me, would you?"

Alison nodded. "Of course, Mom."

"Good girl."

Alison vanished in another quick flash of light. Wechsler gave Alice an amused smile. "You let her-"

"*That* is a conversation for another day, John," Alice interrupted sharply.

"Of course it is." Wechsler leaned back in his chair comfortably. "The Heroics kids are getting a bit too close, don't you think?"

"I doubt that they've figured much of anything out. They're just stopping bank robberies, remember? Sure, they'll probably start to think it's strange that there are more empowered villains running around, but I doubt they'll piece anything together."

"I wouldn't be so sure of that," Wechsler replied mildly. He glanced up at her. "You know my

22

daughter has joined them. She thinks she can hide from me, but I know she's with them. She might be a fool for leaving, but she knows enough about our operations that I find it hard to believe she won't start putting things together eventually."

Alice shrugged. "Then perhaps we should remove her from the equation entirely." She raised an eyebrow. "If you're okay with that."

Wechsler laughed. "Do you honestly think I wouldn't be?"

"Thought I would check. I wasn't sure if perhaps you'd gone soft in your old age."

"We're the same age, Alice, you're only insulting yourself." Wechsler interlocked his fingers in front of him. "And I am nothing like Giada, Austin, and Diana."

"I didn't think *they* were 'like them' until they betrayed us."

Wechsler gave her a small smile. "I don't plan on backing out of his operation, Alice. The Vigilance Initiative will go on as planned, even if *dear* little Tess needs to die. Don't worry, my friend."

"Consider me a business partner, not a friend, John," Alice said as she headed for the door. "After all, I know quite well what happens to your friends." She paused, leaning against the door and looking back at him. "Do you really think your daughter is that much of a threat?"

Wechsler's eyes narrowed. "I think that she could be. If you don't believe me, send one of your security people to try to rough her up a bit. See what happens."

3

Zach "Kov" Carter knocked politely on the brick wall surrounding the Heroics mansion. After a minute of nothing happening, he slid a pair of silver sunglasses out of his pocket and put them on. "Casey," he said patiently.

He heard an irritable sigh in his ear. "It's nine in the morning. What do you want, Kov?"

"Are you going to let me in or not?"

"I don't remember giving you permission to come here."

"You're a pain in the neck, you know that?"

She sighed again, loudly, and then the back door slid open. Zach, smirking slightly, removed the silver glasses and descended into the base.

He met Casey as soon as he stepped into the building. The woman was standing a few feet from the door, her arms crossed in front of her and an annoyed expression on her face.

"I gave you a communication device so that you could call if you needed help. Not so that you could complain," Casey said.

"You wouldn't open the door. And besides, I don't need help from you," Zach replied.

"Fine, next time you get stuck in a prison I'll leave you there."

"And the next time you break into an office like an idiot, I'll leave *you* there."

Casey hesitated. "You'll always need my help."

24

"I could say the same to you, sweetheart," he retorted, grinning.

The word "sweetheart" bought him a death glare, but Zach happily ignored it; sparring with Casey was one of the few good things about being the liaison between the Security Legion and Heroics. He was pretty sure she hated him, but that just made the interactions more fun.

"Do you need something, Kov, or are you just going to hang around irritating me all day?"

"Both. And Casey, please, when we're in the safety of your own base, could you call me Zach instead of my hero name? There's no reason for secrecy in here."

Casey made a quiet hissing sound, which was an irritation level above her earlier scoff, but agreed with a, "Fine, *Zach*, what do you need?"

"We need to talk. Something's going on in the hero community, and it might be bad. Very, very bad."

AJ pocketed his phone as he headed for the elevator, pausing in front of the control room to look in on Cass. She was staring up at the screens, her jacket- covered in bloodstains -hanging off the back of her chair.

"Is that your blood?" he asked hesitantly.

"Nope."

"Oh. Okay. Good." He paused. "Do I want to know?"

"Eh, some guy tried to mug me or whatever. It didn't go well for him."

AJ, deciding not to ask further, started back towards the elevator. When the band on his wrist beeped, he glanced down at it. "Casey wants us in the conference room ASAP."

"Okay." Cass stood and, electing to leave her bloody jacket behind, followed him to the elevator.

Kate and Lori exited the training room and headed towards the elevator as their bands beeped. Kate yawned. "We need to stop getting early morning calls. It kills my sleep schedule." She glanced up and noticed Cass heading in the same direction. "You get much sleep, Cass?"

"Not much."

AJ, next to her, shook his head a little bit too purposefully. "That's a shame. Don't you just hate it when that happens?"

Cass shrugged. "Eh, it's not that bad."

AJ smirked. "I'm glad."

Lori leaned over to Kate and lowered her voice. "Ten bucks says I know why she didn't get much sleep last night."

Kate gave a choking laugh that she hurriedly tried to stifle behind her hand. The two adults paused and looked at them, confused.

"Something wrong, girls?" AJ asked, frowning.

"Nothing at all," Lori replied quickly.

"Any idea what this is about, AJ?" Kate asked, neatly changing the subject.

"Not even a little."

"Then I guess we'll have to just wait and find out."

Alice opened the door to Wechsler's office angrily. "Your daughter beat up one of my most experienced security officers. How? She's a lab rat!"

Wechsler smirked. "She's a lab rat who grew up surrounded by mercenary soldiers. She learned a thing. Or two. Or several."

"I'd be impressed if I didn't want to kill her."

"There is a very large list of people you want to kill, Alice."

"You're just noticing this now?"

"No. Simply pointing it out."

Alice paced in front of his desk. "I think we need to accelerate our plans."

Wechsler's brow furrowed. "Why? Getting scared just because one test subject escaped?"

"Your daughter isn't the only lab mouse who seems to have gone over to the other side."

Wechsler frowned, and then realization flickered into his eyes. "No. Which one?"

"The dark one. I tried shutting her down permanently, but I think she figured out a way around it. It's very likely that she ran off to help *them*. I never could quite control that one."

"Well then," Wechsler said, quietly and dangerously. "We'll have to find a way to hunt down our rogue experiments, now won't we? Accelerate the program, Alice." He stood, turning towards the windows and looking out at the city. "It's time to bring this infestation down."

AJ walked into the conference room behind Cass, Kate, and Lori. He hesitated when he saw Zach. The blond man was seated at the head of the table, leaning back in Casey's usual chair with a strangely subdued look on his face. He was older than AJ but had always acted much less mature. Zach was an upbeat kind of guy, so the fact that he was neither smiling nor poking at Casey meant that something was seriously bothering him.

As AJ sat next to Cass he looked at Casey, who was in the chair next to Zach's and scrolling through her tablet furiously. "What's going on?" he asked quietly.

Casey looked up and set her device down slowly, glancing at Zach before saying, "Some empowered people have been... disappearing."

"Disappearing?" Kate echoed. "What does that mean?"

"Several adult heroes have vanished off the face of the earth," Zach said. "Sensors, telepaths, nothing can find them. At first we thought that some of the empowered criminals were killing them off, but a bunch of them have gone missing, too."

"None of them have been found?"

Zach shook his head at Jay's question. "No, none. Which is odd to me, because the list we have so far from here and the surrounding areas is sixty in the last two months."

"*Sixty* empowered people and we're only hearing about this now?" Casey asked incredulously.

"Most of them were criminals," Zach replied. "We weren't keeping track of them." He rubbed his hands together slowly. "The two most recent to disappear were Ryder "Jetstream" Jefferson and one of your Alumni kids, Clarice "Porter" Wagner."

The Alumni team was the former group of Heroics kids. Now adults, they had all left the mansion and become their own team of empowered people. Clarice, a twenty-six-year-old who, despite her serious demeanor, had dyed her hair pink, had been the team leader.

"Is there anything that we can do?" Justin sounded concerned, which meant that either he had taken these disappearances personally or was seeing them as a way that he could be the hero and show up his sister.

Zach shrugged. "We have no idea. We're notifying all of the teams to warn them and to have them keep an eye out for any signs of the people who've disappeared." He handed Casey a small stack of papers. "This is all of the empowered people who have gone missing."

"We'll watch for them," Casey promised.

As Zach nodded he said, "Good."

The kids left the room after that and headed for the elevator. As Cass and Casey talked about something quietly between themselves, Zach stood and walked out; AJ followed. "Zach! Hold up a second."

Zach paused. "What is it?"

"Jetstream. Ryder Jefferson. I know him from somewhere. He's your best friend, isn't he?"

Zach gave him a solemn look. "Yes, he is."

"I'm sorry."

"So am I."

AJ held out a hand. "Be careful out there, Zach."

Zach accepted the handshake. "You as well."

AJ frowned. "I'm a base person, remember? I think I'll be okay."

"I know." Zach's gaze was distant. "But I have a bad feeling about this one, AJ. I think whatever's coming is going to affect all of us one way or another."

"What are we supposed to do?" Justin asked his sister as he sat on the living room couch.

"We do our jobs and pay attention. And we don't go running off on our own."

Justin scoffed at Kate's response. "What good will that do? We don't know if safety in numbers is even relevant to this situation."

"Don't be such a pessimist, Justin." Kara leaned back against nothing, floating two feet off the ground. "It doesn't suit you."

"This isn't pessimism," Justin retorted. "It's a legitimate concern. We should go looking for them. Go through warehouses to see if we can find any evidence that they're being held somewhere. *Do* stuff. Be proactive instead of looking for thieves and waiting to magically stumble on something."

"Justin, we literally found out about this five minutes ago," Julian said. "It's foolish to go charging into something like this without knowing anything. All of those people were more experienced in their powers than any of us-"

"But I-"

"*Please* don't, Justin," Kate interrupted. "Please, just let it go for today. It's Saturday and so far it's been quiet and I'm tired. Can we just have a day without you causing a fight or an argument or whatever? Please?"

"Fine," Justin grumbled. "But I know I'm right."

"That's generally the problem," Kate muttered to Lori and Kara.

When AJ walked back into the conference room, he saw Cass and Casey staring intently at the corner of the room, where a shadow was moving on its own. After a moment, it solidified into a hooded figure.

"Who are you?" Casey demanded.

"My name is Alix. Alix Tolvaj. Though some in the hero world call me Thief."

"That's not a very trustworthy name," Cass pointed out.

"No, I supposed it's not," she replied simply.

"What do you want, Tolvaj?" Casey asked cautiously.

"Only to help. I think I might know a thing or two about what Kov was talking about."

"Why would you help? And how did you get in here?"

The opening of the hood turned towards AJ. "I can... *listen* to the shadows, Doctor. I can follow them, too. I hitched a ride on Targeter's shadow after I helped her bring down Tank, and it brought me here. I've listened to the shadows and heard quite a few things about these missing people."

"And what do you want for this information?" Casey asked.

Tolvaj's head tilted to one side. "Why would I want something?"

"Because we've never heard of you," Cass said slowly. "And usually people that show up mysteriously with information are thieves looking to sell. Going by your hero name..."

"Don't judge too quickly, Tess," Tolvaj said quietly. "You've never heard of me before because I was never a hero. I was never quite a criminal, either. I was a messenger. But I decided to leave my line of service when I stopped believing in it. I decided to side with you, so here I am."

"Then what do you know?" Cass prompted. "If you just want to help, why not just tell us?"

"All I know is that the kidnapped empowered people are apparently being used for experiments. And the name Cage keeps coming up."

"Cage? Like Alice Cage?"

Tolvaj hesitated. It was hard to read someone without a visible face, but AJ could practically sense that this girl knew more than she would ever say. "Yes, like her."

Cass bit her lip. "Okay."

AJ nodded. "Thanks for informing us," he said.

"If you ever need some backup, flick this on," Tolvaj said, tossing a black lighter to AJ. "It'll always call me." He could almost hear a smile as she said, "And don't worry. It's not bugged or a bomb or anything like that." She gave a loose salute with her right hand and then disappeared into the shadows she had come from.

"Alice Cage," Cass said softly.

"We don't know if it's true."

"Of course it's true, AJ, you know that she's been out to get empowered people for years, though I expected her to simply kill them. This is unusual, even for her."

"If it is Alice Cage," Casey said carefully, "you might need to prepare yourself in case-"

"I know that my father could be involved, Casey," Cass interrupted. "I wouldn't be surprised if he was." She looked at AJ, her metal-gray eyes cold. "This is more his style, actually."

"What is?"

She smiled humorlessly. "It's more his style to make people simply disappear."

4

Tank sank heavily onto his cell bench. He was surrounded by rock, steel, titanium, and barbed electrified wire, a typical cage for someone like him, capable of going through a brick wall without getting a scratch. He stared at the floor, anger covering his face.

"What do *you* want?" he snarled at the shadows in the corner.

The cloaked girl, Tolvaj, appeared at his words. "I need to ask you one question. And it's very important."

"Why would I answer any of your questions?"

Tolvaj wandered over to stand before him. "Because I'm rather like you, Mr. King. I too am a pawn of Alice Cage."

"You don't know what you're talking about," Tank muttered.

"Don't I?" she challenged mildly. "Listen very carefully to my voice and tell me that I don't know."

Tank looked up, shock spreading across his face. "Who are you?"

"Unimportant. Just answer something for me, Mr. King. Did you have powers before you came into contact with Alice Cage?"

Tank paused. "No."

"And will these powers last?"

Tank hesitated again. "Why do you want to know?"

"Call me curious. Now tell me, emphasis on *now*."

He sighed. "Mine have already worn off. She has the ability to make them last longer; she said that she had done it."

"Yeah, she has," Tolvaj mumbled. In a louder voice, she said, "Thank you very much, Mr. King."

"Wait! Since I helped you, and I'm not a threat anymore, can't you get them to put me in a less secure cell?"

The shadows stared at him. "We don't know that your abilities won't come back. And I won't let you put people- even criminals -at risk just because you *might* be powerless."

"But I helped you," Tank snarled.

"Yes, and I don't remember making any particular deals regarding your time in prison in exchange for it."

"You're a thief when it comes down to it, aren't you? A thief of information."

Tolvaj laughed. "I've been called that many a time, Mr. King. How else would I know your name when the people who locked you up don't even have that?"

Tank froze. "I hadn't even... realized it..."

"Yes, well, I'm very good at this, very, very good at finding the piece of information that will keep me well in the loop; it's how I survive. Now if you don't mind, I have some informing to do. Thank you for your time, not that you had much of a choice in the matter."

Before Tank could say anything in reply, the shadow vanished.

While Kate and Julian patrolled the southwest of Caotico City and Jay and Justin patrolled the southeast, Lori, Ray, and Kara headed into the center of town. It was a quiet Sunday afternoon, and group was able to cross over the rooftops without so much as a second glance from the people below. "Is this when I'm supposed to say that 'it's quiet, *too* quiet'?" Ray joked as he adjusted his black gloves.

"If you say that and someone attacks us, I'm killing you in your sleep," Kara replied.

Ray pushed her gently. "I'd like to see you try, kid."

Kara narrowed her eyes at him. "Don't call me 'kid.' You're only a year older than me."

"A year? Aren't you like eleven?"

"*Thirteen*, thank you very much. My birthday was last week; you can't have forgotten that quickly, no matter how dumb you are."

"Well I'm fourteen, so you're still a baby from my perspective," Ray replied with a grin.

Kara punched him in the shoulder, knocking him off of his feet. Ray frowned up at her from his spot on his back on the roof. "Hey, watch your super-strength, would you?"

"I did it on purpose."

Ray stood, his hands sparking with electricity. "It's going to be that way, huh?"

Lori, who had been watching the conversation silently, shook her head and hit them both in the face with rainwater that had pooled on the rooftop overnight. Both Ray and Kara jumped, spluttering and drying themselves off. "Gross, Lori, who knows how long that's been out here," Ray whined.

Ignoring him, Lori said, "If you two don't mind, we're supposed to be on patrol, and I'd very much like to finish our sweep quickly so that I can go home and do my schoolwork."

"Ew, schoolwork."

Lori gave Ray a look. "Don't emulate Justin. He's a bad example."

Ray laughed. "I can't be copying Justin, because he doesn't even know what schoolwork *is*, let alone whether he likes doing it."

Lori hesitated before nodding and shrugging. "Fair enough."

"Justin's not really going to run off to look for the people who have gone missing, is he?" Kara sounded worried as she jumped over to the next roof.

"I don't think so," Ray said. "I don't think he's *that* dumb."

"I think that he would make the decision to go out and start looking, but not on his own." Lori pushed back a strand of her dark brown hair that had gotten stuck under her sunglasses. "He's hot blooded, you know that. Things need to be done *now*, whether that's the best choice or not. But he knows well enough that he can't cover everything by himself. Even if he went out alone, I don't think he'd go poking around in unfamiliar places."

"He's stupid, but not *stupid*, you mean?" Kara asked with a smile.

The older girl laughed. "That's a good way to put it."

There was a flash of red, and Jay appeared in front of them. "Quake and five other criminals are holding hostages on Sutherst Road. Can you guys lend a hand?"

"What, you can't handle it yourself?" Ray said jokingly.

Jay laughed sarcastically. "Yeah, I'll just ask them politely to leave the residence while they hit me in the face with rocks."

"Why not just dodge them like a real speedster? Don't wimp out on us now, Clash."

Lori elbowed Ray in the side. "That's enough. Leave him alone. Now come on; we've got a job to do." She looked at Jay. "Go on ahead. We'll catch up."

Jay nodded and sped off. "When *don't* we have a job to do?" Kara muttered as they headed off towards the street that had been named. She glanced at Lori. "What does the Security Legion even do around here?"

"They handle the north, and sometimes they take the south during school hours."

"There's definitely more of them then there are of us," Kara said. "Can't they at least wander down here once in a while during the rest of the day?"

Ray smirked. "I'll tell Casey to ask Zach."

"Oh, please don't," Lori said quickly. "I hear enough bickering during my day; I don't need those two going at it as well."

"The only 'going at it' those two want to do is-"

"Blackout," Lori interrupted in a warning tone.

"Oh you're no fun."

"Just shut up and keep moving."

38

Ray laughed and started jogging. "Keep this strict leader routine up and you'll give Kate a run for her money."

Kate always found Mondays to be difficult. They signified the first day of school after the weekend, which wouldn't really be much of a problem to her, but for some reason criminals in Caotico City always seemed to like coming out in droves on Mondays.

This Monday in particular was a problem, because Niall wouldn't leave her alone.

Niall Sullivan, seventeen, with black hair and cobalt blue eyes, was Kate's boyfriend. He didn't know about her extracurricular activities, though, and she had always been determined to keep it that way. But the busier the criminals got and, by extension, the busier Kate got, the more difficult it was to keep him out of the loop. Especially now that he was worried.

"Kate, what's wrong? You've been acting weird recently."

Kate shook her head. "It's nothing, Niall. I've just been... busy."

"Yeah, I've noticed. But whatever you're doing is taking a toll. You look tired, all of the time."

"Gee, thanks."

"I'm serious, Kate. You should take a break from... whatever."

"Look, Niall, I..." Kate paused. She wasn't sure she wanted to finish the sentence, but seeing as things were apparently getting worse in her world, she had to. "I think we should stop seeing each other."

That had clearly not been what he had been expecting, because for a long time Niall just stared at her. "What? Why?"

She sighed. "I-"

She was cut off when a man landed out of nowhere next to them. He was tall, thin, and had large, scarlet wings.

"Redhawk," Kate breathed.

"You know this guy?" Niall asked incredulously.

She shrugged nonchalantly. "More or less."

"Oh, she knows me," Redhawk snarled. "She put me in prison!"

"You robbed an armored truck, idiot, I couldn't just let you walk away."

Redhawk smirked. "Well I can't just let *you* walk away. Which is why you aren't leaving here alive."

"Yeah... I don't have time for this. There's a reason that I alone was able to put you in prison so easily." Kate produced a small foldout crossbow from inside her jacket, aimed it at Redhawk, and fired twice. He dodged the first arrow, but the second struck him in the chest and sparked with electricity. He fell to the ground. "Taser arrow, jackass. You really should get a weapon or armor or something. Stop being such a pathetic enemy. How the hell did you recognize me anyway?"

"Sunglasses are a terrible disguise," Redhawk replied through gritted teeth.

"Ah, good point. Honestly I'm surprised no one's noticed that before." She pulled a zip-tie from her pocket and tied his wrists together, then wrapped a thin line of wire around his wings. "I'm sure the cops will round you up on their next sweep."

Kate folded up her crossbow and looked at Niall. He was standing absolutely still, staring at her with his mouth open. She took a deep breath. "We need to talk."

"So let me get this straight: You're a *superhero*?"

Kate continued leading her boyfriend down a secluded path in the park behind the school, staying silent for a moment before answering, "For lack of a better term, yes."

Niall blinked. "Do you have, like, powers?"

"More or less."

"What can you do?"

Kate sighed. "If I shoot at something, chances are that I'll hit it, no matter how small or difficult the shot." She pulled her crossbow back out. "For example, see that leaf falling from that tree over there?"

"Yes."

She raised the crossbow and fired. The arrow hit the leaf dead center and pinned it to the tree. Niall swallowed, looking overwhelmed. "You hit a small, moving object from sixty feet away without actually aiming."

"Yep."

"… That's awesome."

Kate couldn't stop a pleased smile from spreading over her face as she headed towards the tree to retrieve her arrow. "I'm glad you think so."

"You're one of those vigilantes I keep hearing about, then?"

Kate winced. "We prefer the term 'heroes.' Less stigma to it."

"Heroes," Niall echoed quietly. He put his hands in his pockets. "So you spend the time you aren't in school running around in a uniform practically begging for someone to kill you?"

"This is exactly why I was trying to break up with you before that idiot decided to drop out of the sky."

"Let me guess: 'It's not you; it's my enemies,' right?"

Kate looked away from Niall, wincing again. "Listen-"

"No, *you* listen. That's a terrible reason not to have a life! If the bad guys find out that we *used* to date, it'll be just as bad for me as if we currently *are* dating. If you have a legitimate reason to break up with me, fine, but doing so to protect me is bullshit."

His girlfriend looked up at him, her eyes wide. "I thought..."

"You thought that finding out that you have powers would make me want to break up with you? It'll take some getting used to, but you're going to have to try harder than that to get rid of me, babe."

Kate grinned and kissed him quickly, but before she could reply, the band on her wrist lit up. Looking down she pulled out her sunglasses and, slipping them on, asked, "What is it, Control?"

"Alix Tolvaj is back, and she has something very interesting to tell us."

"I'm on my way." Kate pocketed her glasses and looked at Niall, who had a confused look on his face. "I need to go. I'll explain more tomorrow."

"So you're telling us that Cage is *giving* people powers?" Lori asked incredulously. "How does that even happen?"

"She's very good at what she does," Tolvaj replied. "Science is her thing. If there's a way to do it, Cage will find it. Knowing things is what she does."

"And why should we trust you? We can't even see your face!"

Tolvaj turned to Justin. "I know that you don't trust people easily, Archer, but I'm on your side. You'll have to believe that."

"I don't *have* to do anything." Justin stood up from his chair and walked over to Tolvaj. "For all I know, you could be working for Cage. You could be a criminal. You could be the person who's really taking all of those empowered people!"

"I'm not-" She had barely gotten the words out before Justin punched her. Kate was on her feet instantly, pulling her brother away before he could swing again.

"That's enough," Kate said firmly.

"All of you. Patrol. Now," Casey said, standing up. "*Now!*"

The teenagers filed from the room, Kate pushing Justin out as he continued to glare at Tolvaj. As soon as they were gone, Tolvaj put her hand under her hood for a moment; when she lowered it, it was red with blood.

"He actually did hit you?" Casey asked, concerned.

"It's just a bit of a bloody nose," Tolvaj muttered. "It's fine."

"I can take a look at it," AJ offered.

"No," Tolvaj said, a bit too quickly.

"Thief," Cass said softly. "You'll need to take your hood off eventually."

"I can't," Tolvaj replied.

"You'll never get them- or us for that matter -to fully trust you if you don't. You know that. I can tell that that's all you want, but you need to lower the hood first."

"You don't understand," Tolvaj said quietly. "I *can't*. My powers… if I don't wear the hood and sunglasses, I can't see. My eyes can only handle very dim light or darkness."

Casey hit a switch, and the lights dimmed until the only illumination came from the pale glow of her computer. "Could you now?"

Tolvaj hesitated. Then, after a moment, she slowly lowered her hood and removed her glasses. She winced slightly, even in the faint light, but kept her gaze steady.

She looked young, probably in her late teens but no older. She had long, light brown hair. She was pale, with dark gray eyes that were similar to the color of Cass's.

"Wow," Casey said, looking thoughtful. "I hope you don't mind me saying, but you look kind of like you could be a young Alice Cage."

"I imagine I would, seeing as I'm her clone."

"… Yeah, that would do it."

44

Tolvaj looked between the three adults, her eyes full of fear. "I-I would've told you, but... I didn't... I..."

"Relax," Cass said gently, fully aware of the fact that Casey and AJ had both turned to her. "Just relax, kiddo."

"How can I?" Tolvaj looked away, her hands rubbing together nervously. "You hate Alice Cage."

"And you aren't her," Cass said firmly.

Tolvaj took in a breath. "All I want is to help. I don't want anything to do with her anymore. But I didn't... I didn't know how to breach the subject. I didn't know how to handle the questions about who I am."

"Then by all means, help. We'll probably need all the help we can get if people keep disappearing." Casey smiled. "And as long as you don't start acting like Cage, I don't care where you came from."

"Agreed." AJ squinted at the blood on her face. "I'll go get something to help clean that."

"Thanks," Tolvaj murmured.

"And I have an idea for your sight issue," Casey said. "I might be able to modify my glasses design to work for you. You wouldn't need to wear the hood all of the time. Tomorrow morning, come by my lab. I'll go now and see what I can come up with."

As she walked away, Tolvaj turned to Cass. "I don't understand. Why are you all trusting me this easily?"

"All of us have secrets. Problems. Backstories. If all the tales were good, none of us would be here. Sometimes, in this line of work, you need to take risks; sometimes the bad guys are actually the good guys."

Tolvaj glanced over at AJ, checking to see how close he was. She lowered her voice. "You'd know all about that, wouldn't you, Tess?"

Cass swallowed nervously, paling. "I thought you'd used my first name the other day, but I wasn't sure…"

"I know quite a bit about you. Alice did a bit of an experiment. I have the memories of all of the clones she made." She paused. "All the way back to Alicia."

"How much do you-"

Tolvaj interrupted with a soft hiss as AJ walked back over to them. Cass sighed. "It's okay. He already knows all of it."

"All of what?" AJ asked as he handed Tolvaj a towel.

Cass waved a hand at him, brushing him off. She was staring at Tolvaj. "How much do you know?"

Tolvaj paused, wiping the blood off of her face. "I know everything, Tess. What Alice was experimenting with. Why your eye color is identical to mine." Her voice lowered again, almost unconsciously. "What she and Wechsler did to you."

Any color left on Cass's face drained. She took a slow breath, and then said, "Please. Please don't tell the others about… me."

"I wasn't planning to," Tolvaj replied. She shrugged. "What I know is mostly only facts anyway. It's like a horror movie constantly playing

46

in my head. It's not my story, Tess, it's yours and the decision of whether to tell it is yours to make."

"Thank you."

"You don't need to thank me. You're trusting me. That's all I want." An unidentifiable emotion was in Tolvaj's eyes. "Now, if it's alright with you, I'll be going."

"If you ever need, sixth room from the stairs on the right fourth floor is an open bed."

Tolvaj narrowed her eyes. "Why-"

"If Casey is making you glasses, you're officially a part of Heroics. We all sleep here. There's always a room if you need one."

"Th-thanks." Tolvaj vanished.

AJ absentmindedly ran a hand down Cass's back. "Are you okay?"

She gave him a weak but affectionate smile. "Yeah."

"Are you lying?"

"Actually, no."

"Are you sure we can trust her?"

"I don't know. Maybe I'll regret it later. But for now, I don't see a reason to be cold to her. She seems... *scared*, AJ, and I know that feeling all too well."

5

Casey was working in her lab at seven o'clock in the morning when Alix appeared in the room with her. Casey jumped, startled by her sudden presence. "Can you give some warning?" she asked weakly.

"Sorry."

"Have a seat." Casey gestured at the chair off to the side. "I'm almost done."

Alix sat down silently as Casey continued working on the pitch-black sunglasses on her table. "Do you think those will work?" Alix asked quietly.

"I'd imagine so. It's not that hard of a concept. I'm surprised Alice didn't try."

That got a dry laugh from Alix. "Would it make my life easier? Then Alice isn't going to do it."

Casey didn't reply; she simply finished screwing together two pieces and then held the glasses out to Alix. "Give it a shot."

After a brief hesitation, Alix took the glasses, slid them on, and then slowly lowered her hood. There was a moment's pause before the girl grinned. "Hey, I can actually see for a change."

"I'm glad," Casey said, smiling. Alix looked around the room while Casey put her screwdriver away and removed her protective glasses. "I have a question."

The grin on Alix's face faded. "Okay."

"You obviously have worked for Alice for a while. Why come here now? The real reason."

Alix bit her lip, thinking for a moment. "My job for Alice was to deliver information and messages between her and John Wechsler. I'm a faster and more private method than phones or email. Now, I've always known that those two aren't good people. But what was I going to do? I didn't have anywhere else to go. Then I found out that Tess had run off to Heroics, and I started wondering, if someone with her background could find a place here, maybe I could too." She swallowed. "I didn't make up my mind until I went to deliver a message and discovered that John had shot Tess in the chest, just like he had done to her mother. Right then, I made the right choice, and I never went back."

"You're the one who got Cass to the hospital that day," Casey realized.

"Yes," Alix confirmed, looking uncomfortable.

"Does... Does Cass know that?"

"No. It's not a big deal."

"It might be for her," Casey said gently. She shifted in her seat. "You knew Cass when she was a kid, didn't you?"

The girl nodded. "I have quite a lot of information in my head. She's a part of most of it."

"So the question is, is your loyalty going to be with us, or with Cass?"

Alix seemed surprised. "Isn't that the same thing?"

"Normally I'd say yes, but it still deserves an answer."

"Now that Tess is here, she's not going anywhere," Alix replied firmly. "Neither am I."

49

Casey picked up one of the white alert bracelets from a small pile of them and tossed it to her. Alix caught it and looked down at it, confused. "What's this for?" she asked.

"That," Casey said as she turned back to her table, "is your official welcome to Heroics."

"So, what, you guys actually trust me?"

Before Casey could answer, Kate stopped in the doorway. "Casey, I told Niall that I'm a hero and now I want to invite him over."

For a moment Casey just stared at her as the words processed. "Okay..."

Kate raised an eyebrow. "That was meant to be a question."

"Didn't sound like one." Casey finished putting away her tools. "He's only allowed to come if you think he wouldn't mind babysitting the system once in a while. Cass is going to kill me if I make her sit at that computer for 24 hours straight again."

"He's going to go to college for computer science."

"... Is that a yes?"

"Yes."

"Then he can come over."

Kate grinned. "Thanks, Case." She ran off, pulling her phone out of her pocket as she went.

Alix turned to Casey. "Does that sort of thing happen often?"

"What, the teenagers acting like teenagers? Yeah pretty much." Casey sighed. "Oh, I just realized that between you and Niall, I've gained two more teenagers to deal with. This will be fun."

"I wouldn't really consider myself a

teenager," Alix said cryptically.

"What would you consider yourself?"

"Ah... complicated."

Casey laughed. "Fair enough. Now get out of here, I have work to do."

Alix, smiling slightly, stood and headed for the door. Before she got there, Casey called her back. "Alix?"

"Yeah?"

"We'll trust you unless you convince us that we shouldn't. We're trusting folk."

"That's dangerous in this day and age," Alix commented quietly.

"Is it a bad decision?"

"Not in terms of trusting me," Alix said. "Though from what I understand, not everyone is as trustworthy as they seem these days." She let her words sink in for a moment before she gave Casey the same loose salute she had done before and vanished into the shadows.

Kate and Kara were in the library studying when Justin walked in, flipping through something on his tablet. "Hey, have you seen Cass and AJ?"

Kate smirked. "They're 'discussing changes to the control system,'" she said, using air quotes.

An identical smirk appeared on Justin's face. "Ah. I take it that they don't want to be disturbed?"

"I wouldn't recommend it."

Justin laughed. "Do they seriously think that we don't know? Are they trying to use some kind of refuge in obviousness or something?"

"What's to say that they aren't actually having a discussion?" Kara asked, frowning.

Kate and Justin stared at her. "Remind me to explain the concept of 'blatant lies' to you," Kate said.

"... I do know what that means."

Justin grinned. "Not in this context, clearly."

"You guys are both immature."

Kate grinned. "It's not immature to tease someone behind their back for their incredibly obvious 'secret' relationship."

"I'm pretty sure that's the *definition* of immature."

"The definition of immature is 'not fully developed,' to be precise."

"Like your brain and sense of humor?"

"I've trained you well. I'm so proud." Kate headed for the door, mussing Kara's hair as she went. "I'm going to go get a drink. While I do that, you should probably take time to be horrified that you're turning into me."

"I've already thought about that," Kara muttered as she flattened down her blonde hair.

Justin sat down opposite Kara. "Have you seen... *her*?"

Kara frowned at him. "Her who?"

"Alix Tolvaj. Ray say that Casey is letting her stay. *Here*. With us. They're letting her *join*. I don't remember them asking us if she could."

"Justin, last time I checked, Casey's family owns this place. Her mother runs Heroics. I think Casey can do whatever she wants. Alix was downstairs in Casey's lab this morning, and apparently they had a long chat. Whatever was said there, Casey trusts her. We have to accept that, even though you don't want to." Kara shifted her

52

position in her chair and looked back down at her tablet. "I talked to her, too. She seems nice enough. Try giving her a chance. Maybe we can't trust her... I don't know. But for the time being, Justin, just deal with it."

"Yeah, yeah, whatever. And to make matters worse, Kate is bringing her *boyfriend* here."

"Niall? He's coming here?"

"Yeah. He know she's a hero, so Casey gave her permission to bring him here. This place is getting more and more crowded. I hate it."

"Get over it, Justin. Everything changes eventually, that's how it works. The whole Alumni team used to live here too, remember?"

Justin made a noise in his throat. "I liked you better when you were a nice little kid and nothing like my irritating sister."

Kara smile. "I'm your sister too, smart guy. Just not by blood." She kissed him on the cheek. "Calm down, Justin. You'll never get anywhere in life if you don't." She turned and walked from the room.

Niall walked into the Heroics base already overwhelmed. Surprising fact number one was that the so-called "Phantom Mansion" was where his girlfriend actually lived. Surprising fact number two was that there was a secret tunnel under the ground that led to the mansion's basement. Surprising fact number three was that there was a huge base of operations in said basement. He hadn't even gotten through the door before the processing centers of his brain began to shut off.

"How are you doing?" Kate asked gently.

53

"Fine," Niall lied.

She smiled slightly. "Yeah, it can take some getting used to."

"But you grew up here."

"I did, but it wasn't always this high tech. Stephanie didn't really put much into it at first. Casey's the tech wizard; she's the one that really updated it."

"And Stephanie is... your boss?"

"I suppose you could call her that; she's our guardian. There are seven kids who live here, all the orphaned children of heroes. There are houses or apartments in the names of Stephanie, Casey, and our team doctor, AJ. Justin and I go to school listed under AJ's address. Kara, Julian, and Ray go to school across town, each under one of the three addresses. Jay and Lori go to another school, listed under Stephanie's and Casey's places respectively. We're spread out so as to not draw as much attention."

"Smart. Whose idea was that?"

"Stephanie's. You probably won't meet her today. She doesn't really spend much time here."

"I thought you all lived here."

"We do, but Stephanie's... different. She runs this place, but she's not really a part of it."

"Why-"

Before he could finish the question, a redheaded woman, probably in her thirties but not by too many years, exited one of the nearby rooms- which Kate had identified as the control room -and walked over to the pair. After a moment, a man, with black hair and about the same age, followed her. As he walked, the man fidgeted with his tie, but

54

the action seemed more like a nervous tic than a sign of discomfort with the accessory choice.

The two adults stopped next to each other in front of Niall and Kate. Niall noted that when they stopped, their shoulders brushed, but they each gave a small step aside so that there was a good inch between them. He could tell by the faint amusement in Kate's eyes that she had noticed as well, but decided that whatever the joke was, it was none of his business.

"You must be Niall," the man said, holding out a hand. "AJ Hamil."

Niall accepted the hand. "Niall Sullivan."

As he shook the woman's hand, she smiled at him and said, "Tess Cassidy, but everyone calls me Cass."

Niall nodded. "Kate told me about you two. The team doctor and the mission control, right?"

"Yep," AJ said. He nodded back towards the room he had just emerged from. "Want to see the system?"

"Sure!"

AJ and Cass led Niall to the room that housed a large array of computer screens and keyboards.

"What *is* all this stuff?"

"This is our command center," Cass said. "We can see layouts of the city, see where alarms are going off, see where our people are, and, on good days, access security cameras."

"This is cool." Niall grinned. "Could you show me how some of this works sometime?"

"Sure. Come on down once Kate's done showing you around."

"Awesome. This is what you do, then? This is what mission control does?"

AJ nodded and gestured at Kate. "We're the ones who get to send these idiots out to do all of the nonsense."

"And of course there's more than plenty of nonsense around here," Kate said with a grin. "Come on, Niall, let's go upstairs. I'll show you the rest of the house." She playfully shoved past AJ and headed for the elevator.

The two teens had been gone about four minutes when Cass turned away from her computer and stepped forward until she was very, very close to AJ.

He shifted uncomfortably. "What... what are you doing?"

"An experiment," Cass replied slyly, sliding her arms around his neck.

"What... kind of experiment?" AJ asked, swallowing nervously.

"You're cute when you're flustered." She leaned forward slowly, stopping just short of kissing him. "And you're hot when you're frustrated." She smiled slightly. "I wonder how easily you switch between the two."

"That is a terrible idea."

"Really? I don't think so."

"Of course you don't. But the kids could come back any second. You-" Cass interrupted AJ by kissing him.

"I feel like this is going to be easy."

"You're a cruel woman, Tess Cassidy."

"Oh, you know you love it."

"Yeah, but-"

Cass kissed him again. After a brief moment where AJ considered fighting her, he gave in and kissed her back. The kiss became deeper and more intense until the door to the control room slid open again. They practically shoved themselves away from each other hurriedly as Niall stepped into the room.

Niall frowned as they stared at him. "What?"

"Nothing," AJ said quickly, fixing his tie. He cleared his throat awkwardly, trying to slow his breathing down to a normal, or at least less obvious, pace. "What do you need, Niall?"

"Kate was having some problem with Justin. She sent me down here to have Cass show me stuff with the computers. She asked for me to send AJ up if he's free."

Cass was facing away from Niall, both trying not to laugh and to erase the embarrassed flush from her face. She turned back to the teen and nodded. "Oh, of course, yes. Uhm. Right. I'll show you some of the controls. AJ can leave; we'll talk later, right AJ?"

"Right. Yes. Talk later." AJ stayed where he was for a second. "Bye." He quickly walked out of the room, still fidgeting with his tie.

Niall raised an eyebrow at Cass. "Everything okay?"

"Yep. Perfect. Everything's great."

"... Alright..." Still looking confused, and unsure of what he had gotten himself into, Niall walked over and sat in one of the control room chairs.

They had only been at the computer for about fifteen minutes when a communication line opened on the screen. "Cass. Could you come up here please? There's an... issue." AJ's voice was tense, and there was clearly some sort of argument going on behind him.

"On my way." Cass stood and started to head out of the room. "You might as well come along, Niall, though you might not want to put yourself in whatever mess is happening up there."

"Could it really be that bad? I sounded like it was just an argument."

Cass laughed. "You've never seen superpowered kids have an argument before, have you?"

"… No."

"Then you'll learn quickly that you generally don't run *towards* them."

Niall realized fast enough that Cass hadn't been lying. Julian was in the center of the room, telekinetically holding Kate and Justin on opposite sides of the room. Justin was screaming at Kate, gesturing wildly towards the girl that had been introduced to Niall as Alix Tolvaj, the newest member of the team, about which the term "member" was currently being used loosely. Alix herself was standing opposite Julian, leaning against the wall and looking impassively at Justin.

"What is going on?" Cass asked, sounding stunned.

AJ, who had been talking to Jay and Kara, walked over to her. "They found out that Alix is

Alice's clone. Everyone took it pretty well. Except Justin."

"Why does that not surprise me?" Cass muttered. She walked forward until she was standing next to Julian. "Everyone, just calm down, okay? Or I'll have Julian throw you into a few walls."

AJ winced. "Cass, they get enough injuries as it is…"

"Shush you." Cass crossed her arms. "What's it going to be?" she asked, loud enough to be heard over the shouting. When it didn't stop, she gave a frustrated sigh, then yelled, "QUIET!"

Kate and Justin stopped shouting instantly. "What?" Justin snarled in Cass's direction. "We're busy here."

"I've noticed," Cass said dryly. "All of you out, right now. But not you-" she pointed at Justin "-or you." She pointed to Alix who was adjusting her pitch-black sunglasses. "The rest of you, goodbye. You too, Niall."

As Niall followed Kate out of the room, he once again had the feeling that he was locked out of the loop. But this time it was about something much, much more serious than whatever he had witnessed earlier.

"Now, what is the problem?" Cass demanded, glaring at Justin.

"I don't trust it," Justin growled.

Alix gave a quiet, bitter scoff. "*It* has a gender, and a name. You should try using them."

He snorted. "That would imply that you're an actual human being."

59

"What the hell else could I be? Cloning doesn't negate the fact that I am still flesh and blood, and make conscious decisions, and can make my own choices!"

"You were *created*," Justin snarled. "You were made with the sole purpose of being an experiment. You aren't a person, you just pretend to be one! Things end up being experimented on because they *aren't human!*"

He had barely gotten the words out of his mouth when Cass grabbed him by the front of his shirt and violently slammed him into the nearby wall. She started to take a swing at him, but AJ, who seemed to have been waiting for that reaction, lunged forward. He grabbed her arm so she couldn't throw the punch, then put his other arm around her waist and dragged her away from Justin.

"Cass, stop it!" he managed urgently, struggling to keep her from breaking out of his grip.

"He needs someone to punch him in the face," she spat, looking furious.

"I know that but you are not helping the situation! Calm down!"

Cass stopped fighting, but she continued giving Justin a look of pure hatred.

Justin laughed quietly. "Oh, I get it." He brushed at his shirt to fix where it had been wrinkled by Cass's shove. "Daddy used you when he ran out of lab mice, huh?"

AJ would've lost the fight to keep Cass from killing Justin right then but before she could try to break free again, Alix grabbed Justin instead. She punched him hard in the face, threw him to the ground, and from there made him disappear in a shadow.

"Where did you send him?" AJ asked warily.

"The lake," Alix replied calmly, her anger only evident in the way her hands twitched. "I hope he can swim."

"He can."

"Then I don't think I should bring him back." She raised an eyebrow at the man, making the statement a question, and AJ hesitated.

"No, let him get back here on his own. Just double check to make sure he isn't drowning or anything."

Alix grinned and vanished, at which point AJ realized he was still holding Cass, and he slowly let her go. The woman was breathing heavily; the fury on her face was still obvious. "Are you okay?" AJ asked gently.

"… Yeah." She stared at the ground, embarrassment setting in. "Sorry. I… I shouldn't have let him get to me like that."

"He's not exactly the nicest, most tactful person. Your reaction wasn't necessarily wrong, and it certainly wasn't your fault."

"What if he's right, AJ?" Cass asked softly.

"Then hell is freezing over and pigs are sprouting wings." When Cass smiled, he gripped her shoulders. "What your father did to you and what Alice did to Alix does not change a damn thing, and it most certainly does *not* mean that you aren't human. You and Alix are both people who didn't deserve what they went through. It's not something that you should be ashamed of, but that doesn't mean you need to accept it either."

"What Alix went through...." Cass sighed. "Someday I suppose I should ask her about that, shouldn't I?"

"Yeah, I think maybe you should."

6

"I can't believe she threw me in the freaking lake," Justin snarled, throwing a fresh shirt over his head as he walked into the library.

AJ narrowed his eyes at him over the book he was reading. "You're lucky I didn't let her drown you."

Justin made an irritated sound. "It isn't even Alix you're annoyed about. You're always taking Cass's side now."

AJ set his book down slowly. "Taking her side?" He stood and walked forward until he was about a foot away from Justin. "You're an insensitive, bigoted asshole who only cares about himself and isn't smart enough to realize that it's not a good idea to piss of the only person who is both willing and able to help you after you get stabbed by a random criminal. And if that happens again, and I somehow forget painkillers, I hope you think back to this conversation."

Justin snorted, but there was a faintly nervous look in his eyes. "You wouldn't do that. You're a doctor."

AJ smiled slightly. "Yes, because I've been such a model example of a doctor before now."

Justin glared at him. "What is it about Cass, huh?" he asked softly. "You were never this uptight before she got here."

"Two things. One, this isn't me being uptight, this is me calling you out for being a jackass. Two, you should stop talking before you really get yourself in trouble," AJ growled quietly.

"You're a terrible mentor."

"I'm not a mentor. I'm an ally."

Justin laughed. "What's the difference?"

"The difference is that I don't have to care when someone on your own team decides to beat you up."

Justin took a threatening step towards AJ. "We all know that you're only defending Cass so that she doesn't stop sleeping with you. If you weren't so eager to have her tongue down your throat, you wouldn't be giving me such a problem."

AJ grabbed Justin by the collar of his shirt and pushed him up against the bookcase. "You really don't know when to stop," he snarled. "This is your last warning. Do *not* talk like that to me again, or I will end you. Understood?"

Before Justin could respond, his bracelet started to flash with an alert. "Sorry, I have to go," he said with a hint of smarminess.

AJ kept his grip for a long moment before releasing him. Justin headed for the door, but paused with his hand on the doorknob and looked back. "She's not one of us, AJ. Neither of them is. And you can try to defend Cass all you want, but one of these days you're going to see that people like her- people who used to be on the other side? - never truly change." He gave the medic one last arrogant smirk before disappearing down the hallway.

Niall sat down at the kitchen table across from his girlfriend. "Kate," he said, taking a sip from a can of soda, "you never said that two of your mentors were seeing each other."

Kate put her own can down slowly. "Pardon?"

"Cass and AJ." He gave a small laugh. "I, uh, accidentally walked in on them making out. I pretended that I didn't see anything so that I didn't embarrass them, but I actually did." Niall looked up and frowned when he saw the look on her face. "What?"

Kate was smirking. "We, uh... They haven't told us that they're together yet."

"Oh, crap." Niall fidgeted with his can. "You're going to tease them about this, aren't you?"

"No more than I already do." Kate grinned. "Making out? Really?"

"That's the best way to describe it," Niall said carefully, looking uncomfortable.

Kate laughed. "I knew it. I knew they were just as bad as us."

"I got the impression that they prefer the times when no one else is around."

She snickered. "I'm not surprised. I'm fairly certain that they sneak out and go to AJ's apartment when they get nervous about the fact that they live in a building with eight other people."

Niall frowned slightly. "I feel like it's possible that you care a little bit too much about Cass, AJ, and their secret relationship."

His girlfriend shrugged. "It makes things more interesting around here. Plus, Cass has been with us for over a year. For that entire time, it has been so incredibly obvious that they're attracted to each other that it's almost ridiculous. We can all see it. But until they admit it, all we can do is watch as they painfully pretend that nothing is going on. Maybe I shouldn't be so interested in it, but I am. Call it a weird curiosity."

Niall studied her for a moment. "You really do like teasing them. I almost feel bad for them."

"I probably should, too."

Alice Cage was hunched over a test tube when Wechsler walked into her lab. "John, this is a surprise. You don't usually find your way over to my neck of the woods," she said, focusing on the tube and not bothering to look up at him.

"I think it's time for the next step," Wechsler said quietly.

Alice glanced up at him. "The next step? You mean…"

Wechsler nodded. "Release one of them. Let's watch the vigilantes deal with one of their own people."

"Who should I use?"

"Hm. How about the new guy? What's his name… Jetstream?"

"The tornado one," Alice said thoughtfully. "Yes, that would do. Have Alison show you to the release bay. Oh, and John?"

"Yes?"

"Do remember that once you release one, you aren't getting it back."

Wechsler grinned. "Isn't that the point?"

"Yes. And one other thing: I was thinking of sending a few of my security personnel into the Heroics base to rough them up a little. Send Diana, the vigilante community, and those insufferable brats a nice, neat little message."

"You know what happened last time you sent your security near Tess."

"Yes, but I don't *expect* them to get out. Alison's going to drop them in and then leave them there to get beaten up and arrested. The message will still go through regardless."

"This is why we get along so well, Alice."

"And why is that?"

Wechsler smiled. "We don't mind letting people get killed."

Ray looked around the corner of Westin Street cautiously, his hands clenching and unclenching as they sparked with electricity. "Anybody see anything?" he muttered.

"Not a thing. Maybe the others are having better luck across town," Kara's voice said. She was perched on a nearby rooftop. "Are we sure that there was actually a call from here?"

"That's what Cass said," Lori replied. She was at the other end of the street, standing near the water fountain. The streets in this section of the neighborhood were always completely empty at three in the afternoon, as that was the exact time that no one was at lunch and everyone was at work. It made for easy surveillance, because, generally, if you were on those streets you were either a hero or up to no good.

"While we're alone to our conversation," Kara said quietly, "does anyone know what Justin said to her?"

"Probably something mean and obnoxious," Lori replied, sounding annoyed. "He's good at that."

"I feel bad." Kara jumped to another roof and looked up and down the intersecting streets.

"She'll be okay," Ray said as he stepped out onto the street. "She always is."

"Yeah, but somehow that makes me worry about her more." Lori gave a soft laugh. "Hey, do you think that- ack!"

"Lori? Lori!" Ray sprinted down the street, with Kara flying over the rooftops, to where Lori was pulling herself out of the fountain, coughing and using her powers to pull the water off of her body.

"What the hell?"

"What just happened?" Ray asked, holding out a hand to help her up.

"I was hit by... well, I suppose the only way to describe it would be a tornado. But I couldn't see where it came from because I ended up in the fountain."

"Good thing you can swim," Ray said teasingly.

"Yeah, yeah." Lori shook the final few droplets of water off of her hands and frowned at him. "Did you see anything?"

"No. Kara?"

"No, nothing," Kara answered as she landed next to them. "I didn't see anyone at all."

"Which is probably a bad thing," Ray said.

Kara raised an eyebrow at him. "*Probably*?"

"Alright, so, definitely a bad thing. Give a guy a break." Ray narrowed his eyes and looked around the empty street. "Kara, go up high and get a good look around."

"Got it." Kara jumped, but before she could go anywhere she was suddenly surrounded by a whirling tornado the perfect size to trap her in.

"Kara! Are you okay?"

"Yeah, but I can't move."

"The constantly moving air is keeping you from being able to control where you go. That's why you can fly, you know," a voice from behind said. "You manipulate air around your body. It's only different from air manipulation because you can only control it enough to support your weight and maybe the weight of one other person."

Lori and Ray turned around. A man with black hair and blue eyes was emerging from the building behind them. "Wait a second," Ray said. "You're Jetstream, aren't you?"

"That's right," the man said. His voice was tight and sounded like he was in pain.

"Do you want to explain why you're attacking us?" Ray asked calmly.

Jetstream gave a force laugh. "I don't think you'd... believe me."

"Hold on, Jetstream is one of the heroes that vanished." Lori was staring at the man. "You're supposed to be missing."

"Yeah, and I was. I got overpowered." He flinched horribly, his fists shaking at his sides. "I woke up in a warehouse. I can't... really remember much. But other people were there." He made a hissing sound through clenched teeth. "They did this. Alice Cage and John Wechsler. They're... controlling me. They can... control my body... but

69

they can't control my mind. That's why... I can talk. They sent me to kill you." He took two staggering steps towards them. "The band... on my wrist. It's pumping stuff into my bloodstream. I can feel it... making me try to kill you. I'm trying to fight it, but even if I don't it hurts like hell. It's killing me."

"We'll take it off," Ray said urgently. "We'll get it off of you."

"You can't," Jetstream growled. "Only... she can take it off. Cage. She made it. It's... programmed for her. If you try to remove it... it'll kill both of us." He looked up at the teenage heroes and took in a deep breath. "Stop them. Before they... kill us all."

Ray, sensing the danger, took a step towards Jetstream. "What are you doing? Jetstream! Ryder! What are you doing?"

The man, who was now on his hands and knees and shaking with pain, gave a short, sharp laugh. "I'm making sure that I don't kill anyone." Jetstream grabbed the band and pulled at it. He immediately gave one loud scream and then fell forward onto the ground where he stayed, facedown and motionless.

The tornado surrounding Kara disappeared, and she dropped back to the street as Ray ran over to Jetstream and crouched down next to him. After a moment he looked sadly over at Lori and Kara.

"He's dead."

Kate walked into the kitchen and stopped, leaning against the doorway. Cass and AJ were sitting next to each other, just a little bit too close for the size of the table. Each of them was focusing on their tablets, seemingly paying no attention to each other. Cass shifted slightly to get a better view of her device, and her non-dominant arm briefly brushed against AJ's as she moved. AJ's arm turned over, his palm facing upwards. Cass's hand slid into his, their fingers interlocking loosely. From what Kate could tell, they hadn't even realized they'd done it. It was just an unconscious, affectionate act.

No matter how much she teased them, Kate did approve: Cass needed something good in her life, and AJ needed some excitement, and if they could find that in each other, then Kate was all for it. Of course, they also hadn't admitted their relationship to anyone yet. Which, if Kate was going to win the bet between the Heroics crew, would have to wait until they sent out wedding invitations. She didn't have much faith in their ability to admit things out loud.

Kate took a few steps back and purposefully made noise as she walked back into the kitchen, giving Cass and AJ time to shift away from each other. No reason to tease them nonstop, after all.

AJ glanced up at the clock. "Ray, Lori, and Kara are out on a call right now, right?"

Cass nodded "Yeah, they left not too long ago."

He raised an eyebrow at her. "Shouldn't you be working then?"

"Oh, fine, be that way," she replied with a smirk. She got up and left the room, giving Kate a nod as she went.

Kate sat down across from AJ, but he stood up. "Where are you off to?" she asked, pretending to be offended.

"The living room to read. Partially because I want to, and partially because, if you've forgotten, you're supposed to be out responding to a call, too."

"I'm not-" Kate froze. "Aw, crap."

"And now she remembers. You know, you're supposed to be the leader. The leader isn't supposed to forget when she's supposed to be, y'know, *leading*."

"Shut up, smartass," Kate muttered as she ran out of the room.

AJ shook his head. "Kids."

Kate ran past Niall, heading for the elevator.

"Where are you going?" he asked, confused.

"A call."

"Ah. I probably should've guess that, huh?"

"Yeah, probably." She grinned, jogged back to kiss him, and then continued on her way. "You're lucky you're cute."

Niall frowned as he watched her go, an uneasy feeling bubbling inside of him.

Walking down the hallway, Niall paused when he got to the living room, seeing AJ sitting inside. He leaned against the doorway. "Hey, AJ, do you have a minute?"

AJ clicked off his tablet and set it aside, pulling off the glasses that he occasionally wore when using the device. "Sure. What's up?"

"How do you do it?"

AJ frowned. "I'm... going to need you to narrow that down a bit."

"I've seen you interact with the others. You're a... I wouldn't say parental figure; brother is more accurate. How do you watch them go out there every day, knowing that it's possible that they won't come back?"

AJ leaned forward in his chair. "It's hard, I'll admit it, but they need to go: it's in their blood; it's what they do. So I watch them go, and I wait for them to come back, because it's what needs to happen." He interlocked his fingers in front of himself and rested his elbows on his knees. "This is what we do, Niall. We're the home base. We're the ones who have to do the waiting. If you can't handle that, you should walk away while you can."

Niall shook his head. "No. I can handle this. I'm here to stay."

The older man smiled. "Good. Then you just might be able to survive the multiple heart attacks this job causes."

A screeching alarm pierced through the building, echoing from all floors. AJ was on his feet instantly, heading for the door. "Speaking of heart attacks," he muttered.

"What is that?"

"*That* means that somebody's walking around downstairs. Someone without permission to be there," AJ replied as he hurried for the elevator.

Niall quickly followed him. "So what do we do?"

"Go check it out, obviously."

"But... what if they have guns or something?"

AJ laughed. "Cass is down there."

"… Okay…"

"Which means that I need to make sure that she doesn't kill whoever it is before we find out why they're skulking around in our base."

When they got to the basement, Niall found that AJ had not been exaggerating. Cass was leaning against the wall across from the elevators, a bored look on her face. Two men in pitch-black uniforms with assault rifles were lying unconscious at her feet.

Niall swallowed. "I take it that you know the feeling that your girlfriend could kick your ass if she wanted to."

"Every single day. Get used to it." AJ blinked, looking confused, and then frowned at Niall. "And she's not my girlfriend."

"Whatever you say," Niall mumbled under his breath as AJ stepped out of the elevator.

"Are you good?" AJ asked Cass, a worried look in his eyes.

"Of course." She smirked. "Alice continually seems to think that her security guards are better than the security guards that trained me. Hers seem to be slightly more advanced versions of mall security. My father's were all ex-military mercenaries. There's a great deal of difference there."

"Okay, show off. What were they doing?"

"From what I can tell, they were looking for us. I think- bless them –I think they actually thought that the base crew would be easy targets."

She shrugged. "For anything else, we're going to have to wait until they wake up."

"That tends to take a while after you deal with them."

Cass smiled. "Don't be jealous of my superior defense tactics."

"I'm not jealous. I'm concerned for my future safety."

"Smart man."

Niall held up a hand slowly. "Neither of you remember that I'm here, do you?"

AJ cleared his throat. "Uh, right. Niall, help me get these two into the med bay. We can tie them up or something in there."

"A med bay, where there are dozens of pointy objects that they could use if they got the chance to?"

"Okay, smartass, where would you suggest?"

"How about the secret parking garage behind that wall over there?" Niall jerked his head towards the wall next to the control room.

AJ blinked. "That'll do."

Cass shot Niall a grin as she took all of the weapons from the three men. "I'll put these somewhere so that they can't get to them."

AJ leaned towards Niall and whispered, "By which she probably means that she's going to play around with them."

"I heard that," Cass said as she walked away.

Niall smiled as he grabbed one of the unconscious men and started dragging him towards the garage. "You're in over your head with that one, my friend."

"Yeah," AJ said absently, frowning after Cass. He blinked again. "Wait. She's not my girlfriend."

"I know."

The older man narrowed his eyes at him. "You know, Niall, sometimes I think that you know a lot more than you admit to."

"That's because I pay attention, sir."

"Don't call me 'sir.' It's weird."

"Yes, sir." Niall grinned at the annoyed look he got from AJ. "Are you going to help me move these guys or not?"

AJ made a quiet, irritated sound and then helped Niall pick up the man he had been dragging. "I'm going to regret voting to let you hang around here, aren't I?"

"I'm not as bad as Kate."

"That's not saying much."

"I don't think I'm as bad as you."

"That's not really saying much, either."

When Niall and AJ returned upstairs, they were met by a solemn gathering of the others, huddled in the foyer. Lori was hugging a crying Kara, Casey was having an urgent, whispered conversation with Ray, and Alix was standing in the corner, listening to Jay and Julian argue quietly. Kate, pale, walked over to Niall and AJ.

"What's going on?" AJ asked.

"Jetstream- Ryder Jefferson –is dead. He… killed himself. Cage and Wechsler put some device on him that forced him to attack Lori, Ray, and Kara. It was full of cyanide and set to inject him with it if anyone besides Cage tried to remove it. He tried to pull it off himself so that he wouldn't be made to kill."

"Good god," AJ murmured. "Who does that?"

"Cass's father, apparently," Kate said just a tiny bit harshly. "She's not handling it very well."

Cass was standing away from the others, looking shell-shocked and even paler than Kate.

"I'll go talk to her."

Kate nodded. "When she's calmed down a bit, we need her to see if she can pick up any signals from the device."

AJ nodded. "I'll see what I can do. And when you have a minute, someone needs to interrogate those goons that were downstairs. Did Cass tell you about them?"

"Yeah. Julian, Casey, and I were planning on going down in a bit. We just needed to get this mess sorted out first."

"Good." AJ walked over to Cass, whispered something to her quietly, and then led her out of the room.

"Are you okay?" AJ asked gently as he and Cass stepped into the living room. He closed the door behind them and rested a hand on her shoulder. "Cass," he said softly. "Are you okay?"

She looked up at him, and he noticed that her eye color had darkened, a telltale sign that she was trying to block out her emotions. "Look at this," she said, holding up a picture. "Just look at this."

AJ took the picture and studied it. It was of a thick, silver band that looked to be opened at a

77

seam. Tiny, sharp needles covered the inside of it. "What is it?"

"That's what killed Ryder. It's full of a mix of chemicals that forces you to follow the orders given to you when it activates. The chemicals pump into your bloodstream constantly, keeping you from deviating from your mission. You can speak, but it's very hard to control any part of your body. I can't even imagine how much effort he must have put into setting it off." She gestured at one needle that was thicker and sharper than the others. "If anyone besides Cage tries to remove this thing, this needle shoots out into your wrist, pumping a high dose of cyanide into you. You're dead before you hit the ground." She then pointed at several smaller needles that circled the outside of the band. "And these go out in an attempt to give whoever tried to remove the band some cyanide of their own."

"How thoughtful," AJ muttered. "Who comes up with something like this?"

"Cage and my father, apparently," Cass replied icily.

AJ winced. "I'm sorry."

"Don't be. It's not your fault." She gave a scoffing laugh. "In fact, if it's anyone's fault, it's probably mine."

"You've said that a time or two when Wechsler gives us problems." AJ frowned. "How could any of this be *your* fault?"

"Doesn't matter," Cass said briskly. Clearly not interested in letting him pry further, she took the picture from him and narrowed her eyes at it. "We need to figure out what makes this thing work. I'm going to talk to Alix; see if we can't deduce what our parents are planning with this."

She started to turn away, but he grabbed her arm. "Hey."

When she turned back around he rested a hand on her cheek and kissed her lightly. "It's going to be okay. Got that?"

"Yeah." She smiled at him weakly and then quickly walked from the room. AJ just watched her go, then gave a small, sad sigh and followed her out.

Cass glanced behind her to check that she had lost AJ and then sidestepped into a nearby storage closet. She pulled out a small black phone, staring at it for a long moment. Her thumb hovered over the dial button, and then, flinching slightly, she pressed it and raised the phone to her ear.

"Tess!" Alice's voice said cheerily. "How wonderful of you to call."

"That wasn't necessary, Alice."

"You're going to have to be more specific."

"What you did to Ryder Jefferson wasn't necessary," Cass growled.

"Oh, but it was. I got my point across, didn't I?"

"What, that you and my father have no qualms about killing people? I already knew that."

"People die all of the time, Tess. It's not my fault if I decide to speed up the process. In fact, that's why I sent my security people to you with a phone and instructions to have you call me."

Cass laughed. "If you think I'm going to set up a meeting with you so that you can kill me, you're quite mistaken."

"Oh, I think you'll come to me. You should really listen to my offer, Tess," Alice said dangerously. "Trust me when I say that you really don't want to turn me down."

Cass hesitated. "Fine. I'm listening."

Casey stepped into her office and shut the door behind her. Zach was sitting in the chair in front of her desk. He was staring at nothing, his hazel eyes dark and distant. She walked around and sat behind her desk. For a long moment he didn't acknowledge her, and then he looked up.

"How are you holding up?" she asked gently. She didn't like the look on his face.

Zach gave a dry, humorless laugh. "How would you be holding up?"

She hesitated. "Jetstream... Ryder... he was your friend, right?"

"Yeah. My best friend since college. Kind of nutty, but all around a nice guy."

Casey studied him for a moment. Grief had made him somber and serious. His expression, usually a mixture of happy and mischievous, was dull and lifeless. "I'm sorry, Zach. I'm so sorry."

"It's not your fault," Zach protested quietly.

"That's not what I'm saying," Casey pointed out. "I'm just... sorry."

Zach nodded tiredly. "Thanks, Case." He paused, looking like he was trying to figure out a way to say something. "The kids... they're all alright?"

"Why wouldn't they be?"

The man raised an eyebrow. "They watched someone die, Casey. They're kids. They should be taking this at least a little hard."

Casey nodded. "It's rough; I'll admit it. They were attacked by a fellow hero, some of them were forced to watch him die, and now they all have been forced to realize that this is a whole heck of a lot more serious than they ever imagined it would be."

Zach frowned, studying his sunglasses, which he was spinning absentmindedly in his hands. "Everyone has to realize that some day, I suppose," he said.

"Yeah," Casey agreed. "Though that doesn't mean we have to like it."

"I've never seen anything like this before," Alix said. She was standing at a table in the library, leaning over the picture of the band. "I didn't know that she was using tech. She's always been a... biology kind of person. She knows mechanics but I've never seen her use them like this. She only does chemicals so far as they equate to biology."

"The chemical part is where my father comes in," Cass replied. She was seated at the table, across from Alix. She sighed and ran a hand through her hair. "I can't believe it's gone this far."

"What? The partnership between Alice and Wechsler? Please. They've been torturing children for years. What makes you think that they're above this?"

Cass looked thoughtfully up at Alix. "You really do remember, don't you?"

"Yes."

"How much?"

Alix paused. It was hard to tell if she was looking at Cass, with the dark tint of her glasses blocking her eyes. "Enough."

"Do you know how much of… how much of it my father did?"

Alix took in a breath. "Cass…"

"Alix, please. The denial has gotten to the point where I can't remember how much of what happened to me was my father's doing and how much was Alice's. My memory is all over the place."

"I've noticed," Alix mumbled. "You don't even know who AJ and Casey really are."

"What?"

Alix froze. "Nothing," she said. "Nothing. Just thinking out loud."

Cass stood up. "Alix. What did you mean about AJ and Casey?"

Before Alix could reply, a loud, angry voice from outside the room screamed, "Where are they?!"

The door burst open and Justin stormed in, closely followed by Kate, who appeared to be trying to talk him down. Justin glared at Cass and Alix, hate brewing in his brown eyes. "You," he snarled. He walked over and grabbed Alix by the collar of her black denim jacket. "You did this." He shoved Alix back into the wall and then took a swing at her, punching her in the face.

"Justin, stop it!" Kate exclaimed breathlessly. She looked like she had been running after him for a while. "It's not her fault!"

"Like hell it's not!" Justin punched Alix again. The girl didn't seem to even be trying to defend herself. "What's the plan, Clone Girl? Going to send innocent people to their deaths repeatedly? Or is the real army just a whole bunch of you?" He took another swing, but he was so angry that he missed Alix entirely. "Oh, wait, I get it. There are only a *few* of you, but you get to act as the generals, forcibly ordering others to die for your cause!"

Before he could throw another punch, Kate grabbed him and pulled him away from Alix. "I'm sorry," she muttered to Cass. "He found out about Ryder, and... I tried to stop him, but unfortunately that's not very easy."

Cass gave a small nod and moved over to Alix. "Are you okay?"

"I'm fine." Alix moved her jaw around experimentally. "He didn't move my glasses, which is the only thing I was particularly worried about."

Justin gave an insane laugh, struggling against Kate. "You hardly even moved. What, clones can't feel pain? Or were you specifically experimented on until you couldn't?"

Alix gave a quiet, dry laugh. "Look, I understand that you're grieving for your friend, but don't talk about things that you don't understand."

"What don't I understand? I've punched plenty of people before, and not one of them didn't even flinch like you. You can't feel pain."

"Oh, I can," Alix said, her voice colder than ice. "But I've been in much worse pain than can be caused by one simple punch." She took a slow step towards Justin. "Do you know what it's like to spend every single day waiting for the moment

83

when you're going to end up strapped to a table, being pumped full of chemicals that will either kill you or make you a puppet? What it's like to have to find a way to deactivate a sensor imbedded at the base of your skull that's set to electrocute you to death if you betray your masters? What it's like to have the lives of four other clones running through your head? To be able to feel the pain of each of their deaths if you think too hard about them, because even though you didn't live those lives, the brain has a funny way of making you think that you did? What it's like to see in your mind a video on constant replay of a girl- a real, *completely human* child –being put to the brink of death and brought back over and over again because her father couldn't give a damn about her life?"

With each question she had taken a step towards Justin, until she was standing right in front of him. "You think that I can't feel pain? No. It's not that. It's that the pain never *stops*." She took in a breath, looking around at the stunned group as if she had forgotten that they were there. After a brief pause she disappeared into the shadows on the floor.

Justin looked a tiny bit ashamed of himself, but certainly not enough from Cass's perspective. "That was a tad overly dramatic, don't you think?" he mumbled.

Kate released him, blinking slowly. "Cass… do you know what she meant with that last point? About the girl?"

Cass swallowed. "No, I don't."

Kate saw the look on Cass's face, and a horrified expression appeared on her own. "Oh my god, Cass."

"I don't know anything," Cass insisted. She quickly walked towards the door.

Kate hurried over and held the door shut with a hand. "Cass. Talk to me."

"I have nothing to say to you," Cass said quietly, avoiding Kate's gaze.

"Just tell me that the thought that I have in my head right now isn't accurate. Tell me that you weren't that girl."

Cass looked up, her jaw clenched. "I... I can't."

"Cass-"

"I have to go." Cass pulled the door open and left.

Kate sighed and turned back to Justin. He blinked at her. "What? What's going on?"

She glared at him. "You're an idiot, Justin."

"Why am I an idiot?"

"Because you don't understand that you can't go blaming innocent people for things!" Kate yelled. "Alix isn't Alice and Cass isn't Wechsler. You can't accuse them of being the ones that killed Ryder! They're on our side, Justin!"

"Oh, so I'm crazy for trying to protect my team?" Justin took a few steps towards Kate, the anger lighting in his eyes again.

"Protect us from *what*?!"

"From *them*!" Justin screamed. "Wechsler and Cage are trying to kill us, Kate. *Kill* us! They want all empowered people dead, for god knows what reasons. You really think that their kids or clones or experiments or whatever the hell Cass and Alix are wouldn't share the same philosophy? Alix was probably *given* powers so that she could gain our trust and kill us when we turned our backs! And Cass? What's to say that she isn't giving her father access to all of our information?"

"I can't believe this. I cannot believe that you are this paranoid. Cass *died* for us, Justin. She took a bullet in the chest, and her heart stopped. And if she hadn't been taken to a hospital within seconds of that happening, she'd be dead right now instead of helping us fight Cage and Wechsler. And that happened because she refused to tell her father about us." Kate shook her head slowly. "You just don't get it, little brother. Sometimes blood doesn't mean anything."

"I'm starting to understand that," Justin growled. "If you can't see, if *none of you* can see how much of a threat they are, then I don't want to be around any of you anymore."

"What are you talking about?"

"I'm done. I'm done with all of you and all of this. I'll save people myself." Justin turned and stormed out of the room.

Kate gave a long, slow sigh. "This week just keeps getting better and better."

7

The living room was eerily quiet the next afternoon. Kate, looking miserable, was curled up on the couch next to Lori and Kara. Julian, Jay, and Ray were seated on the other couch, while Casey and Cass each took a chair.

"Any word from Alix yet?" Casey asked quietly.

"No," Cass replied. "No one's seen her since she left yesterday." She stood up. "I'm going to go talk to AJ. See if he has any ideas on finding her. I'm not sure if that lighter is one use only, so we might not want to use it just yet."

Kate snorted, a combative look in her eyes. "By 'talk,' do you actually mean talk, or are the two of you going to need a few minutes?"

"The 'tease Cass' setting in your brain never shuts off, does it?" Cass said irritably.

"I suppose not," Kate replied. "I'm just saying. You disappear periodically, together. What are we supposed to thin-"

"OKAY!" Cass yelled, looking frustrated. "Fine! I'm seeing AJ! I have been for over seven months! Are you happy now? Can you leave us alone now?" She frowned. "Wh- Why are you all taking out your wallets?"

Lori stood up and started taking money from each of her teammates. "No reason."

"Are you... Did you *bet* on me and AJ?"

"Technically, we were betting on how long it would take for one of you to admit it, and which one of you would finally do it," Julian said as he handed Lori a twenty-dollar bill.

Cass closed her eyes for a moment. "Okay. This is incredibly wrong. But I do have to ask. Which one of you won?"

"That would be me," Casey said, accepting the stack of bills from Lori.

"Really, Casey? Really?"

"Don't start, sweetheart. I plan on doing stuff like this a lot. You're sleeping with my brother; teasing you is my prerogative. How often *do* you sleep with him, anyway? You're in his room like every night."

Cass flushed. "What... you can't... how..."

Casey laughed. "Wow, flustered Cass is *hilarious*. I should embarrass you more often."

Cass glared at her. "You should be nice, or I'll tell the kids that you've known about me and AJ for over a month. Oh, oops, look at that, I just did."

The kids all looked at Casey, who swallowed. "You weren't supposed to mention that."

"You're betting on my life. I think I get the right to embarrass you every once in a while," Cass said with just a slightly mocking note in her voice.

"You *knew*? Like, you had it *confirmed*?" Jay exclaimed accusingly.

"I... may have had a video call with AJ when he was spending one of his nights at his apartment and talked him into admitting that Cass was also there," Casey admitted. "But the bet was for saying it to the *group*," she added quickly. "I broke no rules."

"You're all unbelievable," Cass muttered. She walked out of the room, leaving them to argue.

Cass found AJ sitting in the control room, looking up at the screens. "Anything happening?" she asked.

"Not a thing." He glanced back at her. "You look like you had an interesting afternoon, though," he said as he took a sip from his coffee cup.

"I may or may not have admitted to the others that we're seeing each other."

AJ choked. "Pardon?"

"I got frustrated and told them. It's been a long week; I wasn't exactly thinking straight." She smiled weakly at him. "Is that okay?"

"Of course. Hell, I was only waiting for your permission to tell them."

"Why would you need my permission?"

He raised an eyebrow. "Cass. I'm not a moron."

She laughed. "Well, okay then." She walked over and sat down in the chair next to him. "Anything on Alix?"

He shook his head. "Nothing. It's like she just disappeared."

"To be fair, she can do that."

"I'm not even getting a signal from her glasses, though. She must've taken them off."

"Why would she do that? They're the only thing allowing her to see in the light without her hood on."

AJ shrugged. "Maybe she needed to put the hood back on."

Cass bit her lip. "Maybe…"

"By the way, did we ever get anything from the goons that were in here?"

She shook her head. "All they did was politely tell Kate that they wanted to go to prison."

"They broke into a mansion that's supposed to be empty. We can't just put them in prison."

Cass gave a small smile. "One of Zach's teammates is a police officer. He convinced everyone that both goons have vocal powers. They can't tell anything because they can't talk."

"They can write though," AJ pointed out cautiously.

"They can, but the teammate is making sure that they don't get any information to anyone."

"Good. We don't need more to deal with." AJ leaned back in his chair. "Casey wants us to start monitoring this thing all of the time, scanning for the missing heroes. I've got tonight's shift, so you're on your own."

Cass laughed. "I'm sure I'll manage." She kissed him. "I need to go talk to Casey about some stuff. I'll see you later."

Cass paused in the hallway, tightly gripping the phone in her pocket as she thought about Alice's deal. She could turn it down. She knew that. She knew that it would be much, much smarter to turn it down. Alice would never uphold her end of the bargain, so Cass would just be dying for nothing.

But Alice would follow through on her threats. She would, and Cass had no doubt that her father would get involved as well. No one deserved that.

She was being stupid, but she had to take Alice's offer. She had surrendered to someone who wanted to kill her once before, and that had ended reasonably well.

Cass closed her eyes briefly, taking in a deep breath. It was the only option.

When the debate over the bet had finished, everyone left the living room but Kate, who stayed on the couch, staring at the ceiling. After a few minutes, Lori wandered back in and sat down next to her, joining her in looking up.

"I didn't see Niall around today," Lori commented.

"He's doing some stuff with his brother."

"I didn't know he had a brother."

"Yeah, Andrew. Twenty-one. He's a firefighter on the East Side. Today was his only day off in a while."

"It's nice that they can spend time with each other occasionally, though."

"Yeah," Kate whispered.

Lori paused for a moment. "Kate, Justin will come back, you know. He's gotten pissed off before, but he always comes back."

"It's not the coming back that I'm worried about. It's what he does when he's here."

Lori frowned. "What do you mean?"

"You've seen what he's like, Lor. He has so much hate, and I can't figure out why. We're all in the same position. We've all been through the same stuff. But he insists that we can't trust anyone from outside this building so vehemently that I just... I don't know. Sometimes I think that he doesn't trust anyone."

"Maybe he doesn't," Lori said gently.

Kate gave a sarcastic laugh. "You say that like it's no big deal."

"It's not a good thing, but it's his problem. It's not your job to worry about it, Kate."

"He's my brother."

"He's *our* brother," Lori retorted. "We're siblings, Kate; you know that. Not by blood, but that doesn't matter. He's not your problem; he's *our* problem. And we have more important ones to deal with. You can't spend all of your time staring at the ceiling and acting like you've shut down just because he picked a particularly bad time to throw a fit."

"I just worry about him," Kate murmured.

Lori patted Kate's knee. "We all do. But he'll be okay; I promise. Now come on. We have bad guys to catch." As she stood up and pulled Kate to her feet, the door opened and a tall, serious-looking woman with brown hair and gray-blue eyes walked in.

"Stephanie!" Lori and Kate exclaimed simultaneously. They hurried over to her.

"What are you doing here?" Kate asked.

The woman looked distracted. "I need to talk to Casey. Do you know where she is?"

"Last I saw her she was down in her lab."

Stephanie nodded. "Right. Okay. Thanks." She turned and walked away, leaving Lori and Kate staring after her, looking confused.

Alice looked up from her paperwork as Alix appeared in a swirl of shadows in front of her desk. "Alix. Long time no see."

"Evening, Alice. Send any more innocent people to their deaths today?"

Alice scoffed. "Not you too. I already got the comments from Tess about that whole Jetstream thing."

"What were you doing talking to Tess?" Alix asked suspiciously.

"We have an… arrangement. But that's none of your concern. How's your situation going?"

"What do you mean?"

"I know you've run away to join Heroics, just like Tess did. I'm surprised they haven't killed you."

"Believe it or not, they're much more reasonable than you are."

"Do they even know how many things you've done to them?"

Alix tensed. "I didn't do anything to them."

"Maybe your body didn't, but at least a portion of your mind did. That would be enough for me."

"Like I said. They aren't you. Why do you think I'm on their side now?"

Alice smiled slyly. "Are you sure they aren't like me?"

Alix leaned against Alice's desk. "I know what you're thinking. I know what you did to those kids. I know what's being done to those kids. If I could stop it, I would. But I can't. Even though I can't, don't think for a second that I'll stand by and let them fight this fight alone." Alix stood straight and turned to leave.

"You aren't here to try to kill me, Alix?"

"No. I'm not giving up hope that we can throw you and Wechsler in prison and leave it at that. I'm tired of death."

Alice laughed. "Well, you're too late for that. There's going to be more death soon."

Alix turned back slowly. "What are you talking about?"

Cass swiveled side-to-side in her chair as she watched Casey work, hunched over one of the pairs of sunglasses. "And that's what I think we should do as far as the Niall situation is concerned."

"Sounds good to me," Casey said distantly, frowning down at the device.

"You didn't hear a word that I said, did you?"

"I heard most of it," Casey protested. She pushed the bridge of her protective glasses up on her nose. "I'm just distracted by my work."

"What are you working on, anyway?"

"I was thinking of seeing if I could work the technology that I put into the lenses of Alix's glasses into contacts. Then she wouldn't need to wear her sunglasses all of the time."

"That would be good for her. And us, too. I don't like not being able to ever see her eyes. It's not that I don't trust her, but it's uncomfortable."

"Out of curiosity," Casey said as she leaned back in her chair, "why *do* you trust Alix? You don't seem the type to trust anyone randomly, especially not someone that close to Alice Cage."

Cass looked down and started playing with the class ring that she wore on her right hand. "Let's just say that I've met people like Alix before. They don't usually end up knowing much about Cage's plans, anyway. Plus, she knows things about... me. If I don't trust her, I might never know just how much she can tell me about my history."

Casey studied the younger woman for a moment. "What happened to you, Cass? Who are you really?"

"That's a story-"

"Good evening, Casey!"

"... That will always be interrupted," Cass finished in a mutter as Stephanie walked into the room. She turned her chair. "Hello, Stephanie."

"Tess," Stephanie said in a slightly chilly tone. "What are you doing here?"

"I... live here?"

"Oh, really? You live in Casey's lab?"

Cass glanced at Casey, confused, then stood up. "I'll... go check the computers."

"Doing your job. What a novel idea," Stephanie said sarcastically.

Cass, looking bewildered, left the room. Stephanie took the chair she had vacated.

"What is wrong with you?" Casey asked. "Why are you always so mean to her? What's she done to you?"

"You'll understand when you're older," Stephanie said briskly.

"I'm thirty-four."

"And I'm sixty-one, so I feel that my point is still valid." Stephanie crossed her arms in front of her. "What's this I hear about an Alice Cage clone?"

"She goes by Alix Tolvaj. She seems harmless, to us at least."

"They always seem harmless, until they attack you." Stephanie thought for a moment. "Get rid of her."

"What?"

"Make sure that she never comes back. Even if you have to kill her."

"*What*? She's just a kid, and besides, she hasn't done anything to warrant that!" Casey exclaimed, looking horrified.

Stephanie narrowed her eyes. "The point, dear, is to stop the threat *before* it hurts you. And don't act like I'm telling you to dispose of an innocent civilian. She's not even human, Casey."

"You sound like Justin."

"Well, occasionally- occasionally, mind you –the boy is right. Now listen to me and do as you're told." Stephanie gave her daughter a stern look and then turned to leave.

"No."

Stephanie stopped at the door and turned back around slowly. "Excuse me?" she asked dangerously.

"I don't know what happened that made you start acting like this, but I utterly refuse to give that order. And if you think for a second that those kids will listen to you over me, you're sorely mistaken. You may have taken care of them, but this isn't your operation anymore. You gave up that job a little over a year ago when you decided that whatever grudge you have against Cass is more important than us. Actually..." Casey stood up and adjusted her glasses again. "It's been longer than that. As soon as the kids actually went out and became heroes, you stopped caring. You left me and AJ to take care of those kids and keep them safe while they were going out there and protecting other people. So you know what? You don't get to make an order like that."

"Casey," Stephanie said patronizingly, "I do know what's best for this team."

"Clearly you don't. If you did, you wouldn't be asking me to have them murder someone."

A dangerous look appeared in Stephanie's eyes. "You don't know what you're doing, Casey. You don't know what she is."

"No, Mom. I think you don't know what *I* am. Now get out of my lab."

Stephanie paused for a long moment, then turned and stalked out.

AJ leaned far back in his chair, yawning. He blinked and shook his head as the shadows in the corner of the room solidified. "I was wondering when you'd show back up," AJ said with a smile.

Alix didn't smile back as her cloak disappeared in darkness. "AJ, I…" She looked down, putting her hands in the pockets of her jeans.

AJ, hearing her hesitation, stood up, all traces of tiredness gone. "Alix, what is it? What's wrong?"

She looked up at him and sighed. "I need to talk to you about Cass."

AJ opened the bedroom door without knocking and stepped inside, closing the door behind him. "Morning, Tess."

Cass, only half dressed, started putting on her shirt. "Uh oh. Real first name. That's never a good sign. What's up?"

"I just had a rather... *enlightening* conversation with Alix about you."

Cass took the time to slowly finish buttoning her shirt before she turned to face him, her expression blank. "Oh?"

"Yes, and she told me about a very interesting deal between you and Alice Cage. Care to comment on that?"

"I don't know what she's talking about," Cass replied, but her façade had slipped into a nervous look.

"Bullshit," AJ snarled, fuming. "You know *exactly* what I'm talking about."

Cass blinked, startled. "I-I've never seen you this angry before," she murmured.

"Yes, well, maybe I'm annoyed that here I was thinking that you were starting to stop hiding things, but apparently I was wrong."

"You don't understand," Cass said quietly.

"What don't I understand? You've been having secret dealings with someone who wants to kill us all!"

"What I do doesn't concern you, AJ," Cass said.

AJ, angry enough that he missed the sad look in her eyes, retorted, "It *does* concern me, dammit! The things that involve you involve me too. That's the concept behind 'being involved with' someone. And what's sad about this is that I'd believe you over Alix any day, I really would, but I can see it on your face! I can *tell* that what Alix said is true.

God-" He turned away and ran a hand through his hair in frustration. "Why? What deal could you possibly make with Cage?"

Cass looked down. "She wants me dead, so... I let her kill me, and she stops sending goons after Heroics."

AJ stared at her. "*What?*"

Avoiding his gaze, she said, "The two security guards that she sent here. Part of what they did was deliver a burn phone. I talked with Cage and she offered me a deal. I go to her, and she stops coming for you."

"That is an awful plan, and she's not going to keep to it."

"I know. But what can I do?"

AJ laughed sarcastically. "How about not going and getting yourself killed?"

"What's the difference, AJ?" Cass asked quietly. "I don't matter. I don't matter to anyone."

"You matter to me," AJ said firmly. "You matter to me, Cass, but if you can't tell that? If you can't see that? Then I can't help you." He turned and walked out, slamming the door behind him.

The early morning air was cold around the Heroics mansion as Cass climbed out of the rooftop hatch and sat down on the roof's edge. She looked out towards the warehouses owned by Wechsler, frowning thoughtfully.

"You shouldn't go, you know," Alix's voice said quietly.

Cass jumped. "I'd ask where you came from, but I guess I know," she commented without looking up at her new companion.

"Everywhere has shadows," Alix replied as her cloak vanished and she sat down next to Cass. "Some more than others."

"That's supposed to be some kind of metaphor, isn't it?"

"No. I imagine that a cave would have more shadows than a beach at noon in the summer.

Cass laughed. "You're a smartass, you know that?"

"Yeah, I've been told that a time or two."

They just sat for a long moment, looking out over the rest of Fuego Village. Cass looked over at Alix. "How do you even know?"

"I know because I've been paying close attention to Alice ever since I left her service. Plus, I know you. You'd sacrifice yourself in an instant if it meant protecting people that you care about."

"How would you know? How do you know anything about me?"

"We grew up together, remember? Or, at least, a part of me did. I probably know more about you than you even do."

"Why don't you tell me some of that?"

Alix smiled. "I can't. You wouldn't want to know it, Cass."

"Just one thing. Just tell me whether my father was as involved as Alice was. Please just give me that, Alix."

Alix hesitated. "Yes," she admitted finally. "Yes, he was."

Cass gave a slow sigh. "Thank you."

"Don't thank me. You didn't really want to know." Alix stood back up. "You aren't going to listen to me, are you? You're going to go."

100

"What choice do I have?"

"… *Not* going?"

"I can't do that. Not anymore. You know I can't."

"Honor before reason. No wonder you switched sides. There's not a whole lot of honor inside those walls." Alix put her hands in her pockets.

"AJ's pissed off at me. Why would you tell him what I was planning on doing?"

Alix studied her for a moment. "I told him because he cares. And I thought you cared, too." She paused. "Though now that I think of it, you might actually be doing this because you care *too much*." She let her cloak reappear from the shadows. "Goodbye, Tess," she said before she disappeared.

As the Heroics team stepped out of the training room, headed for the elevator to get ready for school, Kate grabbed Jay by the arm and pulled him aside. "I need to talk to you for a minute."

Jay frowned. "What about?"

"Justin."

There was a pause as Jay shook his head and looked away. Kate didn't blame him for wanting to avoid the subject, but he was the best person to talk to. Jay was as close with Justin as Kate herself was with Lori, so she pushed forward with, "I know you must've talked to him."

"Yeah, Kate, I have. He's not going off after the missing people on his own if that's what you're worried about."

Kate sighed. "Good."

"Do you really think I would've let him?"

The question caught her by surprise. "I don't know, I just… he's not very easy, yet-"

"You always say that, yet you're the one who always seems to have the most problem with him," Jay interrupted.

Kate gave a scoffing laugh. "Please. Have you missed the way he acts towards Cass and Alix? And he certainly isn't agreeable towards anyone around here, even you."

Jay looked irritated. "His behavior towards Cass is unusual, even for him. As for Alix, sure he's being unnecessarily cruel, but you know how he is around new people. What makes it worse is that he's a narcissist who always has to have someone to blame. At the moment, his targets are the only two people that he has ready access to who, as I'm sure you've noticed, are direct blood relatives to the very people we're fighting."

"That's no excuse to-"

"I *know* it's not an excuse," Jay cut her off in a frustrated tone, "but you had to have handled him wrong if he stormed off and started hiding in Stephanie's apartment."

"I think I know how to handle my own brother," Kate snapped.

Jay raised an eyebrow. "Kate, it's been well established that we're all siblings here. What makes you think that you know him better than I do? I've gone to school with him, patrolled with him, shared a birthday with him, all for my entire life. He's just as much my brother as he is yours, and I think I have pretty good standing to say that you pushing at him isn't going to do anyone any favors."

"Well, that's all well and good, Jay, but I don't know what you expect me to do about it now."

"Nothing. He has to come back in his own time. I'm just letting you know so that this doesn't happen again every time he decides to be an asshole."

"I'll be sure to keep that in mind if he ever decides to stop being a selfish prick and come back home."

"That's exactly what I'm talking about. Countering his bitchiness with some of your own is not going to solve our problems."

"I was being perfectly reasonable with him! It's not my fault that he-"

The sharp sound of Lori clearing her throat interrupted Kate for the third time. The younger girl was standing behind them with her arms crossed, looking over Kate's shoulder at Jay. "Jay, aren't you supposed to be showering before school?"

Jay hesitated, his jaw twitching irritably. After a moment he gave a stiff nod and walked away.

"Are you okay?" Lori asked quietly.

Kate refused to turn to look at her. "I'm fine."

"That phrase should be our slogan."

"I'm *fine*," Kate snarled, rounding on Lori.

"Kate," Lori said in a calm voice. "Talk to me."

"I..." Kate paused briefly, seeming to struggle to speak properly. "I don't know how to do this, Lor."

"Do what?"

"How the hell am I supposed to lead this team when I can't even keep it from falling apart every five seconds? Justin storms off once a month. Ray slacks off and keeps trying to drag Kara off with him. Half of the time I don't know where the hell Jay is. The only people I actually feel I can rely on 100% are you and Julian, which is really convenient because I'm pretty sure the others are much more likely to listen to the two of you than to me. And to make matters worse, *I don't know what I'm doing.* How do you lead a team of superheroes? Hell if I know. I can't even get better than a C in my management class, so clearly I'm terrible at leadership in general. Add in the fact that my powers are practically useless and you get someone who should absolutely never have ended up in command of a superhero team."

Lori frowned. "First of all, your team is made up of teenagers. Now you know what it feels like to be Casey, Cass, and AJ all of the time. Second of all, they listen to you. The only reason it seems like Julian and I get more respect is because I'm basically the team mom and Julian is the oldest. As far as your C in management, you get Cs in everything, because you push yourself so hard outside of school that your grades suffer. You're a good leader, Kate. As good as a sixteen-year-old girl possibly can be." She rested a hand on Kate's shoulder comfortingly. "Everything's going to be okay. Nothing's going to happen. Justin will come back, and we'll figure all of this stuff out, and then you'll see that you can do this."

8

Cass stepped into Alice Cage's office, and the door slid shut and locked behind her. She gave a quiet, humorless laugh. "What, do you actually think that I'm going to try to leave?"

"No," Alice's voice said as her image appeared on a screen on the wall. She was smirking. "You'd die before you let me kill your little friends."

"That's the deal, isn't it? I surrender, and you call off your dog."

"Yes, that's right." Alice snapped her fingers, and in a flash of light Alison appeared, leaning against a wall a few feet from Cass.

Cass raised an eyebrow. "Well," she said slowly, "I know that's not Alix."

"No, this is Alison. Alix's twin."

Cass looked at Alice, her eyes wide. "T-Two of them?"

"That's generally the idea of twins, yes." Alice smiled. "Alix might have betrayed me, but Alison here never will."

The teenager's gray eyes were blank as she looked at Cass. "Shall I do it then, Mother?"

Cass snorted. "Mother? Really?"

"Quiet, girl," Alice snapped, and Cass wasn't entirely sure which one she was talking to. "Our deal is sealed, Tess Wechsler. And you'll die."

"Fine then," Cass said. "Already died once, what's the difference?"

Alice gave a chilling grin. "There's a great deal of difference this time, I believe."

The screen next to hers lit up, and Wechsler smiled at Cass from it. "Hello, *dear*," he said.

Cass tensed immediately, but she refused to look at her father's screen. "What do you want?" she spat.

He continued smiling pleasantly. "To watch." He leaned back in his chair. "You know about Jetstream's death, yes? We kidnap the vigilantes before we do anything to them, because those bands only work if we have access to the controlled being's DNA."

"And as I'm sure you'll remember," Alice continued, "we have *plenty* of samples of your DNA from when you were one of our test subjects." She nodded at Alison.

Realization punched Cass in the gut, and suddenly she knew exactly how she was going to die. "Oh, no," she said quietly. Before she could react, Alison moved forward and grabbed her, twisting her arms behind her back.

"The deal, if you remember, is that *I* don't go after your little band of vigilantes. It says nothing about *you* going after them."

Alison clamped a silver band around Cass's left wrist and then backed off, letting her go. Cass stared at the band, fear in her eyes. "You know, I thought I was smarter than this," she said with a weak laugh. "I totally should have seen this coming."

"Yes, I'm actually embarrassed by you," Wechsler said. "I didn't realize you were *this* stupid."

Cass opened her mouth to say something, but before she could there was a chilling *shink* sound, and she instead gave a scream of pain. A thick line of blood dripped out from underneath the band.

Wechsler gave Cass a cold smile. "There is now a high mixture of chemicals pumping into your bloodstream. And as you can tell, this is generally a very painful process."

"Normally we add some painkillers to the mix to make it less uncomfortable," Alice said. "The only reason Jetstream was in pain when he attacked your group is because he was a tad allergic to the chemicals, plus he was fighting them."

"But for you, we decided not to add any of those painkillers," Wechsler said gleefully. "Children that don't behave deserve to be punished, after all."

"You're a real son of a bitch, you know that?" Cass said tightly.

"Don't talk about your grandmother like that. She was a lovely woman."

"Go to hell!" Cass screamed, finally looking at Wechsler's monitor and glaring at him. She could feel the chemicals coursing through her, and she could tell that she was slowly losing control of her own body.

Wechsler's smile didn't waver. "No thank you. I have better things to do. And so do you. Alison, if you would escort our guest back home? She has some superhero wannabes to murder."

Alison leaned against the railing of a catwalk that stretched over the walkway in one of the Cage warehouses. A small bit of darkness flashed in the corner of her eye, and Alix leaned next to her.

"It's been a while, sis," Alison said.

"Not long enough," Alix replied.

Alison smiled. "Still bitter at our mother?"

"You have no idea." Alix lowered her hood, flinching only slightly as her contacts adjusted to block the light. "Care to tell me why Alice was giving bank robbers powers?"

"No. Besides, that project is finished, anyway."

"I doubt that."

The white-cloaked girl watched as a gun shipment was loaded into crates. "What do you really want, Alix?"

"Where is she?"

"Who?"

"Don't play games with me, Alison. Where is Tess Wechsler?"

Alison frowned. "Tess Wechsler? I don't know."

"You're lying."

"And you're a traitor." Alison gave her a sideways glance. "So I don't think I need to tell you anything."

"Listen to me!" Alix said, forcing Alison to turn and face her. "That woman has done nothing wrong! She doesn't deserve whatever her father is going to do to her! Now *where is she*?"

Alison shook her head slowly. "She's at the mansion."

"Bull. Tell me the truth."

Her twin gave a sly smile. "You aren't listening, Alix. *She's at the mansion.*"

A horrified look appeared on Alix's face. "You didn't. They didn't."

"Oh, yes we did."108

Alix punched Alison in the face, looking furious. Alison dropped down to one knee, holding her face. "I'm ashamed that we're related even in the slightest," Alix snarled. "I am nothing like you. Like *any* of you. And you will never be anything like me."

Alison laughed as she stood, completely ignoring the blood dripping from her nose. "Don't you understand? I don't *want* to be anything like you. Why would I want to be a weak, backstabbing idiot? The shame is all mine."

Alix, shaking with anger, took a threatening step towards Alison, but before she could do or say anything, she froze, looking at something that Alison couldn't see. "AJ," she whispered, and she vanished back into the darkness.

AJ, seated at one of the computers, glanced up at Cass when she walked into the control room. As he returned his focus to what he was doing, he said, "If you want me to apologize for calling you out on your stupid plan, it's not going to happen."

"Please shut up," Cass said, her voice wavering. "Please just shut up and run."

"What?" AJ looked up, frowning. He noticed three things immediately. One, Cass was close to tears. Two, her gun was in her hand, gripped so tightly that her knuckles were white. Three, a thick silver band was wrapped around the wrist of her dominant hand. He stood up slowly. "Oh, no, Cass," he whispered. "Oh, god no."

She was shaking horribly, visibly forcing herself to stay still. "Stop. *Talking*. And. Run!" she hissed through clenched teeth.

109

"Just let me think!" he shouted, running a hand through his hair quickly and nervously.

"You-You realize that I c-can kill you, right? You wouldn't... wouldn't stand a chance against me, eve-even without this gun. No o-offense, but I... I think I could beat you... in a fight." Her voice had started to break and stammer from the effort of keeping the gun pointed at the ground.

"No offense taken. I've been aware of that since day one. Do I look like I could win a fight against *anyone*, let alone someone who can have a jacket covered in blood and no one says a damn thing about it?"

She gave a small, strained laugh. "Please don't... don't make me laugh when I'm trying to k-kill you."

"Seems fair enough."

"Listen to me," Cass begged. *"Listen to me.* We b-both know what this thing will... will do to me. What it will... make me do. P-P-Please just go. Just... go. Don't make me die kn-knowing that I've killed you."

"Shut up, Cass. I'm not going anywhere."

"You st-st-stubborn i-idiot!" she exclaimed. *"Why?"*

He grinned at her. "Idiot is right. The solution's been staring us in the face this whole time."

"What?"

He pulled Alix's lighter out of the inside pocket of his jacket and flicked it on. In a second, Alix appeared in the room in front of him. "Let me guess. Cass?" she asked. AJ nodded, and Alix turned around, noticing that the woman in question was in the room with them. "Ah. Right."

"Alice Cage can remove the band, Alix. Think that being her clone is good enough?"

Alix shrugged, looking uneasy. "I can't be sure, AJ. It might work. It might kill her."

"I'm dying a-anyway," Cass said with a faint laugh in her voice. "But i-i-if it doesn't... doesn't work, it will... kill you... too."

Alix shrugged again. "Eh, I've died before."

She started to head forward, but Cass yelled, "MOVE!" Her arm flew up, and the gun started firing. AJ ducked behind the desk, and Alix disappeared into the shadows. After a few seconds, the clip was empty, and the gun stopped. "AJ, are you okay?" Cass asked desperately.

"I'm fine," AJ reassured her, standing back up. "Let's try not to do that again."

"Alix!" Cass yelled. "Do it! Now!"

Alix reappeared next to her. "This is going to hurt," she said to Cass.

"Can't hu-rt more than it already d-does," Cass replied with a weak smile.

Alix smiled back and, with a determined look in her eyes, put her hand on the silver band. Cass gave a scream of pain. Alix grabbed her before she hit the ground as she fell forward, out cold.

Cass opened her eyes slowly, blinking as the fuzziness started to clear from her brain and she was able to tell that she was in her own room. She looked around slowly, noting that a thick bandage was wrapped around her left wrist. She also saw

111

that Alix was sitting in a chair to the right side of the room.

Alix gave her a sympathetic smile. "Well, I told you that getting that thing off of you would hurt."

The woman sat up slowly, flinching when she put weight on her left arm. "You didn't tell me that it would hurt so much that it'd knock me out."

"You had painful chemicals pumping into your bloodstream, and I had to take about fifty needles out of your skin simultaneously without letting you bleed out. Not many people would be able to stay conscious during that."

Cass nodded slightly. "How long was I out?"

"Four hours."

"Damn. Less than I expected, though."

"Yeah, I'm a bit impressed by that."

Cass smiled briefly, hesitated, then murmured, "I-I didn't hurt anyone, did I?"

"No, you didn't. You got pretty damn close to killing AJ, but he's fine."

"Is he still mad at me?" Cass asked in a quiet voice.

"He's still acting like he is, at least," Alix said gently. "But I wouldn't put much stake in it. You should've seen how upset he was when you passed out."

"Do you know where he is?"

"The control room, I think. You should go talk to him. And do *not* remove that bandage."

"Don't worry; I won't. I really have no interest in seeing the damage that fifty needles does."

AJ, hunched over a computer screen that had bullet holes in it, looked up as Cass walked into the control room. He immediately turned back to the broken screen as he said, "You're up and about quickly."

"Yeah. I think my body is so used to recovering from bad chemical mixes that it doesn't bother me as much anymore. I'm surprised that my blood isn't classified as a type of acid."

AJ didn't react to the joke, staring at the screen. Cass sighed. "AJ, please talk to me."

"Why should I?" AJ asked bitterly.

"Dammit, AJ, I tried to deal with Cage to get her to stop chasing you all. That's what I did. It was stupid, and I should've known how badly it would go, but I was trying to help."

AJ took in a slow breath and turned to face her. "You just don't get it, Cass. This isn't about what kind of deal you made with Cage. I never thought that you were going to turn on us. It was never about betrayal. It was about truth, and trust, and understanding your effect on other people."

"I don't-"

"You could've *died*, Cass," he interrupted, standing up. "You could've died, or you could've killed someone, and we would've never known what was happening because you went off on your own."

"I didn't, though."

"That's... That's not the point," he said exasperatedly, closing his eyes and pinching the bridge of his nose. He shook his head and went back to disconnecting the shot pieces of equipment.

"Nothing overly bad happened. I mean…" She trailed off, sighing. "Look, AJ, I didn't tell you because I didn't want to. I didn't want you to know what I was doing, because I knew that you'd try to stop me. Obviously for a good reason, because apparently sometimes I am utterly, utterly stupid."

"That you are." AJ turned back around. "I was scared, Cass. You want to know why I was so angry? That's why. I was scared."

Cass stared at him for a long moment. "I'm sorry."

"Yeah," he said quietly, avoiding her gaze.

She took a small step towards him, looking guilty. "Are we good?"

He looked up at her steadily. "We never weren't."

9

Alison appeared in Wechsler's office. He and Alice both looked up. "You could have knocked," Wechsler commented, looking as if he didn't really care either way.

"Would you like me to leave and come back?" the girl growled.

"Oh, not very friendly today, I see," Wechsler said simply.

"What happened?" Alice asked before Alison could say anything in reply.

"Cassidy didn't kill anyone."

"I'd say that she was a disappointment, but that's not exactly news to me." Wechsler leaned back in his chair. "Did *anything* interesting happen?"

"A few things, yeah." Alison knotted her hands behind her back. "First of all, I thought you might like to know that your daughter has a boyfriend."

"Well that *is* interesting." Wechsler leaned forward in his chair again. "Do we have a name?"

"He's the medic for the Heroics brats. AJ Hamil."

"Hamil…" Wechsler murmured. He smirked and looked at Alice. "Perhaps I should pay the man a… visit."

Alice smiled but didn't say anything to him. She waved a hand at Alison. "Continue."

"Secondly, Cassidy didn't die from the band because Alix removed it."

"Alix?" Alice echoed, frowning.

Wechsler's eyes narrowed. "I thought you took care of that… problem."

"She got rid of her kill switch."

He scoffed. "Well that was poor planning on your part."

"What I don't understand is how she removed the band," Alison said. "I thought only you could take it off, Mom."

Alice scoffed. "Oh, please, Alison, you can't really be this naïve. Alix figured it out months ago."

"Figured *what* out?"

"You aren't human," Alice said patronizingly. "You are a clone. *My* clone. I only created you so that I had someone to do my work for me. That is why Alix can do things that only my fingerprints and DNA can do. She- like you –is identical to me."

"What? But… But Mom…"

"Remember when I told you that I'm not your mother, so you needn't call me Mom? When I said 'needn't' I meant 'don't do that.' You aren't my kid. You have my blood, but that's just a necessary side effect of cloning. You are a clone, with a built-in self-destruct in case you ever turn on me. So a word of advice? Don't follow Alix's traitorous path."

"Wh-why didn't you *tell* me?" Alison asked, her voice cracking.

"I thought it might distract you. But you aren't necessary at the moment, so it doesn't matter at all currently. Go do something useful, won't you?"

"I-I… but…"

"Leave, now," Alice said, giving Alison a humorless smile.

Alison, looking stunned and near tears, disappeared in a flash of light. Wechsler took a drink from his glass. "That was harsh."

"This coming from you."

Wechsler smiled. "I didn't say it was a bad thing. In fact, I approve."

Alice shrugged. "It was about damn time she figured it out." She rolled her eyes. "Honestly, sometimes I think that the cloning process removes some of the intelligence that they should've gotten from being identical to me."

"If there was more than one woman with your intelligence, Alice, the world would be doomed."

Alice laughed. "Brown-nosing for a reason, John?"

"I need a favor…"

Casey looked up as Stephanie walked into her lab. "Wow, twice in three days. This must be a new record," she said dryly. "What do you want, Mother?"

Stephanie sat down. "I heard that Tess almost go herself killed."

Casey nodded. "Yeah, she did. Alix helped her." She narrowed her eyes. "Which wouldn't have been possible if you had had her murdered, but since it was Cass I guess you wouldn't have cared anyway."

"No, I suppose I probably wouldn't have."

Casey shook her head. "What do you want?" she repeated.

"I had to pick up a few things from my room, so I thought I would come down and say hello."

"Well, you have. Hello, goodbye." Casey looked back down at the item on her desk. It was a black plastic box inside of a clear glass box.

"What is that?" Stephanie asked quietly.

"Chwyth-seed oil," Casey replied. "One heck of an explosive in this high of an amount, but Kate was saying something about putting a much smaller amount in the tips of her arrows to combat people like Tank who aren't affected by her normal ones."

Stephanie stared at the box for a moment. "What could the amount you have there do?"

Casey laughed. "Blow up half of a city block, probably? That's why it's in two boxes like this. You really don't want anything setting it off."

"Hm."

Casey glanced up at her. "What?"

"I think I might need some of that."

Casey frowned and repeated, "What?"

Stephanie pulled her taser gun off of her belt and fired it into Casey's chest, sending the younger woman to the floor. "I said that I need that," she said to her unconscious daughter.

"She took your explosives and left?" Ray asked as he sat down at the conference room table.

Casey nodded, rubbing the spot just under her collarbone where the taser dart had struck her. "Yeah, and if you don't mind me saying, it's really pissing me off."

"I can't exactly blame you," Julian muttered.

"The question that needs to be answered right now," Jay said, "is why she took it."

"I've been asking myself that," Casey replied. "I just have no idea."

A flashing light on the wall screen indicated that a video call was trying to connect. Kate hit a button on her chair, and the screen turned on. Stephanie was standing in front of a nondescript white wall, obviously using the video call function on her wristband.

"Mother, what exactly are you doing?" Casey asked, sounding annoyed.

"I'm fixing something that I did a long time ago," Stephanie responded quietly. "Back when Stephanie Cabot wasn't my name."

Casey blinked, confused. "What are you talking about?"

Stephanie sighed. "I was born Diana van der Aart."

Realization and shock flickered in Cass's eyes as she looked up quickly at the name. Stephanie gave a small smile. "Yes, I thought you'd recognize that name, Tess."

"But... *why* do I? I recognize it, but I don't remember it, or anyone having it."

"Memory manipulation is funny that way," Stephanie said. "You can erase the memory itself, but it's very hard, nearly impossible, to erase the visceral reaction to it."

Casey tilted her head to one side. "Memory manipulation?"

"It's my power." Stephanie put her hands up to her eyes and pulled out contacts, changing her eye color from gray-blue to the same metallic gray that kept showing up. "Starting when I was in college, I was in a group along with John Wechsler,

Alice Cage, Tess's mother Brooke Cassidy, and your parents, AJ. We were experimenting with a variety of things having to do with the vigilante menace. One experiment involved giving people temporary powers. I did the experiment on myself, which is why my eye color matches Alix's and Tess's. We've all been used in experiments created by Alice or John. For a time, I had the power of memory manipulation. I used it when AJ's parents and I had a falling out with Wechsler and Cage and left, so that I could erase AJ's and Casey's memories of ever having even met them."

"Wait," AJ said, looking overwhelmed. "You're saying that…"

"You, Casey, and Tess grew up together, yes. That's why I was always so cold and distant to Tess. I was afraid that she'd break through her own mind-wipe and recognize me. I didn't have as much time to erase Tess's memories when we made the final break, so I never did know how well it worked."

"Apparently quite well," Cass said dryly.

"It's also why I was determined to get rid of Alix. Not only do I not trust anyone with Alice's DNA, but I also wasn't sure if Alice had implanted memories into her head of me."

"Why now?" Casey asked, staring at her mother. "Why are you telling us all of this now?"

"Because I won't get another chance to. Alice's security system turned on, so I'm kind of stuck here."

Casey stood up slowly. "Stuck *where*?"

"In on of Shade Security's factories."

"Shade Security as in…"

120

"Yes, AJ, Alice Cage's company. I used Casey's explosives to set the place to blow up."

"Wha- *Mother*!"

"Sorry, Casey. This is something I had to do. If all of this is going to hell, I had to blow up the last pieces of evidence pointing to me and my involvement in John and Alice's plans."

Casey gave a dry laugh. "Even after all of this, even after admitting to us what you are, you still aren't doing any of this for us."

"Of course not. I still want vigilantes to be destroyed. I just don't want any scandal to destroy the image I've worked so hard to obtain."

"If you're dead then you won't need to worry about it."

"Oh, but I will. Don't try to save me, Casey. It's already too late."

"Then explain one thing to me," Casey said, sounding furious. "If you're going to die, then explain one thing. If you hate vigilantes so much, why start this? Why create Heroics?"

"AJ's parents wouldn't let me kill them, but I had to do *something* with those children. Their parents were all killed in our experiments. If we had let them roam, they would've ended up killing people just like all vigilantes do."

"You're unbelievable," Casey whispered. "You are truly unbelievable."

"We all are." Stephanie's gaze shifted to Cass. "I do want to apologize to you, Tess."

"Apologize? To me?" Cass gave a dry laugh. "It's *Casey* you owe the apology to. She's the one whose life you're ruining."

"Yes, but your life is the one that I've already ruined." When Cass frowned, Stephanie continued, "When I erased your memory, I had the opportunity to take you with us. To save you from being a future experiment. To give you a life away from John's schemes. I probably should've taken you away for the sole reason that I knew for a fact that he had murdered your mother when she tried to stop his experimentations on you. But I left you there. It wasn't my place. It was your father's right to do with you as he pleased. But I feel that I should at least extend an apology to you, given the circumstances."

Cass's eyes were cold. "I'm not taking an apology from you."

"And I wouldn't even if you offered me one," Casey spat. "You're a monster, you know that?"

Stephanie's gaze traveled over all of the Heroics kids. "Says the woman who provides technology for monsters." She shrugged and looked at AJ. "Oh, and I suppose I should give you a bit of an apology too."

"Oh?"

"Yes. Several years ago I decided that I wanted to get Alice and John to stop hunting me. So I gave them something in return."

"Let me guess," AJ said slowly. "My parents."

Stephanie shrugged. "I did actually feel bad about that one, though. They were my friends. They just happened to be worth more than me."

"In more ways than one, I'd imagine."

122

"Don't act like that, Casey," Stephanie said. "They were just as involved in the beginnings of those experiments as I was." She looked at something behind her and then smiled at the camera. "I have to go." She hit a button, and the screen turned off.

Stephanie, trapped in an electric cage in the middle of a hallway in Alice's warehouse, smiled as Wechsler approached her. "John. It's been a while."

"That it has, Diana. How are the vigilante brats?"

"As defiant and annoying as ever." She put her hands in her pockets. "Going to let me out now?"

"… No."

The woman's smile faded. "You can't leave me here."

Wechsler smirked. "I'm pretty sure I can."

Stephanie swallowed. "We were a team once. Friends once."

"You betrayed me twice, and you're blowing up one of the warehouses of someone else that you're betraying. I know where the Heroics team is based. I know where my daughters are. I have inside sources for other information that I might need. I have no use for you. You can't hand others over to save yourself this time, Diana." He turned. "You know, from what I understand, Austin and Giada weren't cowardly enough to try to bargain their way out of death when you turned your back on them, even though I expected them to be the weakest members of the Vigilance Initiative. I would never have guessed that the coward would be you, Diana."

"Go to hell."

"You'll be there before I will." Wechsler started to walk away.

"You'll be joining me sooner than you think," Stephanie yelled after him, her voice like ice.

Wechsler didn't look back. "I doubt that."

The Heroics group sat in the conference room in silence for a long time. In the distance, they heard the rumble of an explosion. There was another quiet moment, and then Casey put her head down on the table and started to cry.

10

The next day, the only story on the news was the explosion at the warehouse. Some reporters claimed terrorism, others suggested insurance fraud, and a select few thought that it was simply an accident. Alice Cage made an announcement that her security agents were working on figuring out what had happened. There was fury in her eyes, but her statement was spoken remarkably calmly.

As one news station started playing her speech for the fourth time in an hour, AJ glanced at Casey and slowly turned it off. Casey was seated in a chair in the living room, staring blankly at the floor, while Alix hovered awkwardly near the other chair.

"Casey," AJ said quietly. "I'm sorry."

"There's nothing for you to be sorry for," Casey said hollowly. "This is her fault. Everything." She paused. "You know, I never got along well with her. I always knew that there was something there, something that I didn't like. I always thought that she didn't actually support us and what we were doing. Though I never could've imagined just how far that went." Casey paused again, her hands clenched in tight fists. "You knew, didn't you? You always know."

For a brief moment the other two didn't seem to know who she was talking to, but then Alix said, "I did. Yes."

"Why didn't you say anything?" Casey asked, a note of accusation in her voice.

"It wasn't my place to. For all I knew, she'd changed. She was helping you all, after all. Who was I to accuse her of anything?"

"Diana van der Aart," Casey whispered. She gave a short laugh. "I don't even know my own name."

Alix shifted uncomfortably, and Casey laughed again. "Let me guess. You do?"

"No one in this room- no one in this *building* -has the name they were born with. Tess and I are the closest, since our legal names are still Tess Wechsler and Alix Cage. But the rest of you? It's all lies."

"What's my name?" Casey's voice was quiet but firm.

"I don't-"

"*What is my name?*"

Alix hesitated briefly before saying, "Robin. Robin van der Aart. AJ was Anthony Sadik. As for the kids, I don't know. Their names were lost a long time ago. I know that their first names were assigned to them based on comic book characters with similar powers. I'd assume that's where their surnames came from as well. Your parents came up with that idea, AJ, which is why I wouldn't be surprised if the same naming convention applied after they ran. The kids were supposed to be experiments just like their parents, which is why they vary so much by race. Alice and Wechsler needed to know whether racial differences would affect their formulas." She shrugged. "I don't know everything. Some stuff was probably edited out of my memory by Alice."

"You sure do know enough, though, don't

you, clone girl?"

The girl opened her mouth to say something, hesitated again, and then murmured, "I'm sorry I couldn't be more help, Casey." She took a step back and disappeared into the shadows.

AJ crouched down in front of Casey. "Are you okay?"

She looked at him, her gaze solid. "Yeah, I'm okay. I shouldn't have done that. Alix didn't do anything wrong."

"I'm sure she understands." AJ smiled slightly. "I'm just glad you're okay."

"Are *you* okay?"

"Yeah. Yeah, I'm good."

Casey sighed and cleared her throat. "There's never a dull moment in our lives, is there, brother?"

"Not usually." AJ stood. "Oh, by the way, Zach's on his way over. He wanted to talk to you."

The woman scoffed. "Who says I want to talk to him?"

AJ smiled, thankful to see shreds of Casey circa two days prior shining through the sorrow. "You deny it, but you want to talk to him a lot more often than you'd ever admit."

"Don't play this game, AJ," Casey warned. "You'll lose that fight every day with Cass around."

Her adoptive brother laughed. "Well, for the time being Cass is busy in the control room, so at least she won't have to listen to it. If you don't meet Zach voluntarily, I'll make sure he can find you when he gets here. You both lost people recently; you can talk about your feelings."

"Woohoo," Casey said dryly. "Do you and

Cass talk about your feelings?"

AJ laughed. "That's not exactly the easiest thing in the world to do."

Casey played with her watch for a moment. "Y'know, Cass was the one who told us about you two. But I've never heard you say anything on the subject. About you, and your feelings."

"I don't really need to," AJ muttered.

"You'll need to, eventually. You can talk to me whenever you decide that you do. I'll listen."

AJ hesitated. "You really want to know how I feel?"

"If you're ready to tell me."

"She's a former enemy and the daughter of the guy trying to kill all of us. She's chronically sarcastic and practically incapable of properly showing emotion. She has near-crippling insecurity, nightmares that haunt her even when she isn't asleep, and anger issues that may or may not have been caused by experimentations and chemicals that may *still* be filtering through her bloodstream." He turned back around to face her. "And even with all of that, I care more about her than anyone else I've ever met. And I'm not sure she actually knows it."

Casey leaned forward. "Cass may be emotionally idiotic, but she's not blind. She knows."

"How could you possibly know that?" he asked quietly.

"Two reasons," Casey said as she stood up. "One, I've seen your interactions and I know that you love each other whether or not either of you will admit it out loud." She looked down at the watch on her wrist, which had lit up with an indicator that let her know that Zach had arrived. She stood and headed for the door.

"What's the second reason?" AJ asked as Casey reached for the doorknob.

As she opened the door and began to step through, Casey glanced back at him. "The second reason is that she told me." She flashed him a quick grin and then vanished.

Kate walked into the control room and paused. Niall's legs were sticking out from under one of the computers, and a quiet muttering of curses were coming from him. She walked over to him and lightly kicked his foot. There was a *thunk* sound, and Niall cursed louder. Kate winced. "Sorry."

Niall slid out from under the counter, rubbing his head. "It's okay."

Kate sat down backwards on one of the computer chairs. "What are you doing?"

"One of the computers was acting funny. I think it encountered a problem when AJ was disconnecting the stuff that was shot up and connecting the new stuff. I told Cass that I'd try to fix it."

"Where *is* Cass?"

"Went to get coffee," Niall replied as he slid back under the desk. "I suggested that she add alcohol to it. From what I hear it's been that kind of week."

Kate laughed and then fell quiet, watching as his feet moved around irritably as he worked. After a moment, she said, "Are you okay with all of this?"

There was a pause. "What do you mean?"

"You kind of got pulled into this mess, just because of me. You're in danger even though you're only acting within the base, and being here can't be a picnic. This crew isn't really easy to get along with."

He slid back out, frowning up at her. "They're fine. Everything's fine, Kate. Really. Where's this coming from?"

"I just don't want you to feel like you're being forced to be here."

"I chose to be here, remember?"

"I know. I just…" She sighed. "I love you, okay? I don't want you to get yourself killed just because I brought you into all of this."

"I love you, too. That's why I'm not going anywhere." He spun the screwdriver in his hand, smiling. "Now, can I go back to work, or are you going to ask more dumb questions?"

Kate smiled. "Oh, shut up."

"I'm pretty sure that's what I'm *trying* to do." Grinning, he maneuvered his way back under the computer.

Kate laughed and kicked his foot again. "Jerk."

As she walked out of the control room, Alix stepped out from the shadows near the parking lot. Kate gave a small smile and headed over to her. "Nice of you to stop by."

"I'm always here. You just can't always see me."

"That's creepy, Alix."

She shrugged. "I don't sleep, so I just kind of... wander. It's not like I'm *watching* you guys. I'm just around."

"You don't sleep?" Kate asked.

"Not much. Too much in my head," Alix replied as she pulled off her sunglasses.

Kate blinked. "What are you doing?"

Alix frowned. "What do you mean?"

"Your glasses."

"Oh." Alix laughed. "Casey figured out how to put the light protection in contacts. My sunglasses are no different from yours now, and I can actually take them off."

"Cool." Kate studied the other girl for a moment. "You know, I never knew. Stephanie was right. Your eyes *are* identical to Cass's."

"There's one specific chemical that Alice and Wechsler used in all of their mixtures prior to five years ago. Once it goes into your bloodstream, it alters your eye color to this metallic gray. It's always been the same color, and it always happened. I don't know why. It just... is."

AJ walked out of the med bay and gave them a quick wave. "I'm heading out. See you tomorrow."

"See you tomorrow," Kate repeated, giving him a nod.

Alix frowned. "Where's he going?"

"AJ and Casey each go to their 'homes' twice a month to check up on the places and make sure that no one's suspecting that no one actually lives in either apartment." Kate smirked. "Oddly enough, Cass occasionally disappears from here on nights that AJ's out."

Alix laughed. "That doesn't surprise me in the slightest."

Kate gave her a sideways glance. "You know, I was wrong about you."

"Oh?"

"When you first came here I figured that you would be either an emotionless drone or a spy. But I'm starting to realize that you're neither. You actually have a sense of humor, and I'm beginning to doubt that you'd turn on us." Kate narrowed her eyes. "You have a surprising level of loyalty towards Cass, too."

Alix hesitated. "When Cass and I were little... okay, when Cass was little and when the other clones were around... we always knew what was happening to the other. The experiments were always done on both of us. Alice's clones were never around for more than six years, so they used the clones and Cass so that there was always an age difference between the two test subjects. The clones always died. Cass never did. I don't know if the cloning process meant that the clones were weaker than average, or if Cass was just stronger. Cass always lived. I always died. But I was the lesser being. I don't have a problem with being a clone. I really don't. I don't even care that I'm Alice Cage's clone, because I know that I can think for myself and I know that at heart I'm not her. But..." She sighed. "It hurt, okay? What they did to us. It always hurt. A *lot*. And I can't help but feel that maybe she should've been the one to die, because if she had then she wouldn't have had to go through that anymore. Maybe it should've been me. Er...

132

one of Alice's clones. I keep forgetting that none of those memories are mine."

"Don't sell yourself short, Alix," Kate said quietly. "*Neither* of you should've gone through that. You aren't lesser just because you're a clone. And don't think like that, either. Maybe wishing that Cass hadn't gone through what she went through is a good thing, but thinking that she'd be better off dead is not. She's safe now, more or less."

Alix nodded. After a moment, she awkwardly said, "Have you heard from Justin yet?"

Kate shook her head. "No. This is the longest that he's been gone."

"That's probably my fault."

"Shut up. It's his fault. If he doesn't want to get over it, then that's fine. It's his problem."

"What if he's…?"

"Been captured? No. I've been keeping an eye on him. And I saw him in school today, which is interesting since he hates going there. He must really be desperate to stay away." Kate shrugged. "He'll come back eventually. Probably at the worst possible time, knowing him."

Alix glanced towards the parking lot. "Good."

"Why do you keep doing that?"

"Doing what?"

"Ever since AJ left you've been glancing at that garage. What's wrong?"

"I…" Alix shook her head as if trying to clear it. "I don't know; I just have a bad feeling."

"Your shadows trying to tell you something?"

"… Yeah," Alix replied hesitantly.

"Why don't you go check on him?"

"Yeah. I don't know if it's AJ, though. This feels like it might be coming from either Shade Security's secondary warehouse, or one of Wechsler's buildings."

"Go ahead and take a look. I'll check the control system and see if anything is pinging."

"Okay," Alix said, still looking conflicted. She took a step back and disappeared into the shadows.

AJ shut the door of his apartment behind him. He locked it absent-mindedly, staring down at the pile of mail in his hand. He tossed the pile onto a nearby table and looked up. John Wechsler was standing in the middle of the room, his hands interlocked behind his back, facing away from the door. "Oh, that's not good," AJ murmured under his breath.

"Good evening, Dr. Hamil," Wechsler said brightly as he turned towards AJ.

AJ adjusted his tie nervously. "Do I know you?"

"Oh, I think you do." Wechsler walked towards him, stopping only a few feet away. "And from what I hear, you're dating my daughter."

AJ's eyes narrowed. "I'm not sure what you're talking about."

Wechsler gave a quiet laugh. "Don't play dumb with me, Doctor. I know who you are."

"I highly doubt that you know anything about me, Wechsler," AJ retorted, realizing that pretending not to know the man wasn't going to do any good.

"I imagine that I do. After all, I knew your parents once, boy."

AJ swallowed. "I'm aware of that."

"I didn't have the pleasure of killing them myself. I suppose I'll have to make up for it by killing you."

"Out of curiosity, why now? You seem to have known who I was for a while. So why now?"

"Actually, I didn't know that you were that particular child until Alice did a very thorough search on you. I got your name from Alison Cage. She was watching to see whether Tess managed to kill anyone, and figured out that you were together based on the aftermath."

Wechsler moved forward quickly, grabbing AJ and slamming him into the wall. He pulled out a knife and placed the blade against AJ's throat. "For my daughter to fall for anyone is impressive. But for her to fall for *you*, the son of two people that I really, really wanted to kill? It's like my birthday has come early. It's so useful, really, especially since my daughter doesn't usually play well with others."

"Can't imagine why, given what you've done to her."

Wechsler gave a small smile and put pressure on the knife, causing blood to slowly start dripping down AJ's neck. "Ah, sarcasm. I see what you have in common, besides both of you being people whose mere existence pisses me off."

"You have issues." AJ took in a sharp breath as the knife pressed deeper.

"And you apparently have a death wish," Wechsler whispered. "You're lucky that I want you to die slowly, or you'd be dead already."

"You never answered my question," AJ said. "Why now?"

"The deal that Tess made with Alice was simple. She surrenders, and Alice doesn't make Alison take whomever Tess cares about the most in Heroics and hand them over to me to do with as I please. Obviously, if we had taken interest, we would've figured out pretty quickly that that person is you. And I guarantee that Tess knew that. She also knows what happens to people when I get my hands on them. It's generally not a very pleasant death."

AJ tried to push away from Wechsler, but the older man slammed him into the wall again and pressed the knife even deeper. "Let's do an experiment. I use this knife to force you to leave this building with me, and then we go back to my lab and I use you to find out how much pain the human body can take before the heart just gives out."

Suddenly the knife disappeared from Wechsler's hand. "That sounds like a very interesting experiment, Mr. Wechsler, but unfortunately I think it should remain in the realm of the hypothetical."

Wechsler looked behind him. Alix was standing just a few feet away, her arms folded across her chest and a disapproving look on her face. "Why don't you let AJ go before you're the thing that's disappearing?" she suggested threateningly.

"Alison!" Wechsler yelled as he shoved AJ to the ground. There was a flash of light, and he was gone.

"Well, that was certainly enjoyable," AJ said dryly as Alix helped him to his feet.

Alix frowned at his bloody neck. "I bet. That looks fun. We should get you back to the base before you bleed all over the place."

"That's probably a good idea."

Alix put a hand on his shoulder, and they both disappeared in shadows.

11

Niall sat down in one of the chairs in the control room. "There's so much stuff to learn here," he said.

Cass chuckled. "Yeah, I know. I picked it up pretty quickly, but that's something I've always been able to do. In general it's a lot."

"Are you okay with me imposing on your job here?" Niall asked.

She seemed surprised. "You aren't imposing. Hell, the more people we have around here to help, the better for me."

"Easier to have time to spend with your boyfriend?" He smiled slyly.

"Oh shut up. You're only here so you can spend more time with Kate."

"Fair enough." Niall leaned back in his seat. "Is she okay? She seems… bothered. More than I'd expect even given the situation."

Cass sighed. "She's had a long month, between Alix and you and Justin and the disappearances and this whole thing with Stephanie. For her it's worse than for the others, because she has this belief that she's supposed to take all of the weight because she's the leader. She doesn't, but she'll never acknowledge that."

"I'm not sure how to help her."

The woman smiled at him. "The fact that you care is helping, Niall."

"Why are you so good at giving advice but so bad at taking it?"

"I don't know what you mean."

"I'm sure."

Before Cass could respond, Alix appeared in the doorway, her hands covered in blood. "Uh... Cass, could you go to the med bay for a minute?"

"Just bandage it. It's fine, but I can't do it myself."

Cass gave AJ a slight smile as she examined the cut on his neck. "How exactly did you manage this?"

"Ran into a... friend."

She laughed. "Not a very friendly friend, huh?"

"Not exactly, no."

Cass's smile faded. "AJ, when you're a liar like me, you tend to notice when bad liars are trying to fool you."

"I'm not lying," AJ protested, avoiding her gaze.

"Lies of omission count, y'know." She shifted slightly, forcing herself into his line of sight. "AJ. What happened?"

AJ swallowed and hesitated. After a moment, he admitted, "It was your father."

"My... my *father* did this?"

AJ winced. "I didn't want to just flat out tell you like this, but..."

"No, no," Cass said icily. "It's good that you did." She prodded the gash on his throat a bit too forcefully with an antiseptic.

"Ow," AJ muttered.

"... Sorry." Cass sighed. "I just... I get frustrated by the things that he does."

"Frustrated is probably an understatement."

"Har har."

"I'm not joking, Cass. He pisses you off, and it's more than understandable. He technically *killed* you, for god's sake."

"Yeah, and from the looks of things he tried to kill you, too. Which is probably my fault. He found out about… about us, and he's taking his anger at me out on you."

"I never said that," AJ said softly. "What makes you think I would?"

"I-I…" Cass turned his face away from her, so that she could conveniently both get a better look at the cut and avoid looking him in the eye. She cleared her throat and neatly changed the subject. "You're just lucky that Alix showed up."

"That kid has a weird sixth-sense for when one of us is getting murdered."

"You mean for when *you're* getting murdered."

"Point."

Cass shrugged. "I think she's been keeping tabs on Wechsler and Cage for a long time now. I think that's how she finds out when we're in trouble. She puts those shadows of hers to good use."

"That she does." After a pause, AJ said, "You're deflecting the conversation, Cass."

"I don't know what you're talking about."

"That's kind of the point." AJ pulled back so that he could look at her. "Cass."

"We need to bandage that gash before you start bleeding all over the floor again," Cass said, still not meeting his gaze.

"Cass, please look at me."

She hesitated before looking up. "What do you want from me?" she asked quietly.

"I want to know why you're so adamant to take the blame for this," AJ replied.

"He's my father," Cass said helplessly.

"By blood, maybe, but he was never exactly fatherly towards you. I don't think it counts."

"You just don't get it, AJ," she said, standing up to walk over to the supply cabinet.

"Then explain it to me."

"Why do you care?" Cass exclaimed, spinning back around to face him. "Why do you care so much, AJ?"

"I…" He faltered. "I would tell you, but I don't think you want to hear it."

"Try me."

AJ swallowed, looking nervous. After a brief pause, he said, "I think I'm in love with you."

Cass stared blankly at him for a moment. Her mouth moved silently as if she was trying to say something but couldn't. After another moment she gave up and went back to the closet.

"I shared," AJ said lightly, watching her. "Does this mean you're going to?"

"Uhm, I-I… uh…" Cass buried herself in the cabinet. "Yeah, sure, whatever, in a minute."

AJ frowned. "You're… you're *flustered.* I didn't know you were *capable* of being flustered."

"Learn something new every day," Cass muttered. After a minute she turned back to face him. "I should've killed him."

AJ, who had been staring curiously at her, blinked and shook his head. "Pardon?"

"You asked why I blame myself for the things that my father does. It's because I should've just killed him." She sat back down and started bandaging the cut.

"If I remember properly, you didn't have a chance to do that because you were too busy being dead."

"That's not what I mean. The day before I went back to him, he called me. I was stupid. I knew that my phone was protected from his trace, so I answered it. He asked me to go and talk to him, which I decidedly turned down. Then he told me that in order to 'preserve their experiments,' he and Alice had put trackers in me, and the clones. He said that he could activate it at any time to find the Heroics base, and if I didn't want him to just start bombing everywhere I ever went, I needed to go and talk to him. I should've known that it was a lie, but I couldn't take that risk. I wouldn't have put it past him to have actually done it, so I had to make sure." She gave a bitter laugh. "When I went to him he told me that I was a disappointment. Then he shot me in the chest." She shrugged. "I woke up in the hospital two days later. Nobody knew what had happened, and somehow the hospital had been convinced not to call the cops. I don't know how, and I don't know why I didn't just report the attempt myself. I guess I was concerned with whether they'd interrogate me about why I was there in the first place. I was worried that they'd keep picking at strings until they led back here."

"You've told me this," AJ said. "I know what happened. I spent those two days trying to figure out what had happened to you."

"Yeah," Cass said softly. "But… I should've killed him. I should've just walked into the room and shot him in the head. It would've saved us all a lot of pain and problems."

"You wouldn't have. You couldn't," AJ said quietly. "You're a fighter, Cass, but you aren't a murderer. You're a better person than that. That's the difference between you and your father." He smirked. "And you're much better looking too."

Cass grinned. "Wow, Hamil, that was like actual flirting."

"Was it?" he asked innocently.

"Yeah, it was." Cass leaned back. "You're done. Now you can stop bleeding all over everything. Why can't you just get punched like a normal member of Heroics?"

"Well, you know, *somebody* needs to be the one with the injuries. Though as it's my job to fix them, it's not very helpful when that person ends up being me." AJ rested his hands on his knees so that he was at eye-level with her. "Wechsler told me about the full details of your deal with Alice."

Cass's jaw twitched. "I figured that there was some reason behind why he'd suddenly decide to attack you now."

"You could've told me all of it, Cass. You don't trust me?"

"I do trust you."

"And what's that like?"

"Absolutely terrifying," Cass replied honestly.

AJ gave her a small grin and kissed her. "Good. Some fear that isn't related to actual potential death is good for you once in a while." He held up his wrist, indicating the flashing light on his band. "And now Casey is summoning me." He stood up and headed for the door.

"Hey, AJ?" Cass said before he walked out.

"Yeah?"

"... I think I'm in love with you, too."

AJ flushed slightly and fixed his tie. "Well... good." He started to say something, looked down at his wrist, and then quickly walked out.

Cass shook her head as she watched him leave, then gave a quiet laugh and followed.

Julian dodged out of the way of a weighted ball thrown by Jay, then used telekinesis to throw it back. As Jay sped out of the way, Julian continued redirecting the ball towards him until it flew down low, hitting Jay in the legs and sending him sprawling to the floor of the training room. Julian grinned. "Tag, you're it."

"Very funny, Jule," Jay muttered as he got to his feet. "I almost beat you that time."

"Buddy, you will never outrun me." His grin turning mischievous, Julian mentally brought two weighted balls in front of him. "Especially when I'm actually using two balls."

"You cheating jerk!" Jay picked up a ball and tossed it back and forth between his hands. "Oh, it is so on."

"Not right now it's not, boys," Lori said, walking into the room just as Jay was winding up to throw the ball.

"Aw, but Lori! He deserves it!"

"Funnily enough I don't care. Kate wants us. We have a patrol to do, remember?"

"Fine. Just give us one minute. That's all it'll take to pummel this guy."

Lori tried to look stern but failed, smiling slightly. "Not a chance. Come on. Suit up."

As she turned to leave, she spotted Alix getting off of the elevator. "Hey, Alix, are you joining us?"

"Of course," Alix replied. She had her sunglasses on and was fidgeting with them. "I just need to ask Casey something about my contacts."

"Okay, good. Meet us at the town center."

"You've got it."

Lori and the two boys ran off towards the locker room to change into their Heroics uniforms. Alix headed towards Casey's lab. She was almost there when someone appeared in front of her. Her sunglasses were ripped from her face, and a bright light was quickly shown in her eyes. Alix gave a fast yelp of pain and fell, but before she even hit the ground, a hand grabbed her arm, and she vanished in a flash of light.

Julian pulled his jacket tighter around him, thankful that his colors were white and gray. That way, when his vest wasn't visible, it was much easier to blend into the normal civilian crowd on Main Street. Kara, next to him, wasn't quite as lucky- her maroon pants and orange boots had made at least four people ask her if she was going to the college football game that night.

"Sometimes these outfits suck," she muttered.

"You're the one who picked orange and maroon."

145

"Orange doesn't really go with much."

"*Maroon?*"

"I watch college softball okay?!"

Julian shrugged. "Whatever."

Kate jogged over to them. "Hey, have either of you seen Alix?"

Julian and Kara exchanged a glance and then both shook their heads. "No, I haven't," Julian said. "Why?"

"Lori said that she was going to join us, but that was half an hour ago and neither of us have seen her. I think something's wrong."

"She's *Alix*," Kara pointed out. "She kind of does what she wants."

"I don't know," Julian said warily. "Kate has a point. We might not have known her very long, but she doesn't seem the type to promise to be somewhere and then not show up."

Kate sighed and looked around, fidgeting. "I don't like this."

Alix groaned and opened her eyes slowly. Her sunglasses were back on her face. She blinked and sat up. She was sitting on one of the catwalks in Alice's secondary warehouse.

"Welcome back," Alison said, leaning against the railing a few feet away. "You were out for a while. I didn't realize light was *that* dangerous to you."

"There's a reason I wear these things," Alix muttered, tapping a finger on the side of her glasses.

"I suppose that makes sense."

"What's going on, Alison? If you wanted to talk, you could've just asked."

146

Alison's eyes were ice cold and furious. "I don't want to talk."

"Well... then..."

"I'm here to destroy Alice Cage. And *apparently*, in order to do that I need to kill all three of us."

Alix held up a hand. "Alison, listen to me."

"*No*, Alix! You're a manipulator just like her! We're the same as her!"

"You can't seriously believe that."

"Go ahead and check the DNA. We're her clones. You've always known that."

"Yeah, I have. What's the difference, Alison? We're still people. No matter what we were created from, we're still us."

"My entire life was a lie. For nineteen years, I believed that I was Alice Cage's daughter."

"Six years," Alix corrected quietly.

Alison gave a dry laugh. "Oh, that's right. Sped up aging and false memories. I'd almost forgotten just how much of a fake person I am."

"Stop it," Alix said harshly. "Stop it, Alison. So you're a clone. So what?"

"You don't get it, Alix. I could probably figure out a way to deal with being a clone. But *her* clone? *Her's*?"

"This is ridiculous," Alix growled. "You followed her perfectly when you were her daughter. What difference does it make if you're her clone? It's practically the same thing, you hypocritical moron!"

"Shut up! Just shut up!" Alison waved her hand and Alice fell onto the catwalk from a flash of light.

Alice looked up. "What the hell are you doing, Alison?" she demanded.

"Killing you. For good."

"Are you serious?"

"I already pointed out the logic flaws," Alix said.

Alice glared at her. "Apparently not well enough, shadow girl."

"Stop talking! Both of you!" Alison yelled.

"What are you hoping to gain here, Alison?" Alice asked angrily, ignoring the command.

"I'm ending this clone cycle before it gets out of hand and you end up having an army of yourself attacking everything." Alison pulled out a detonator. "I'm going to burn this place to the ground just like the last one. And all three of us are going to be in it."

"Alison," Alix said slowly. "I think you might have triggered some sort of mental breakdown…"

"I'm fine," Alison said with the type of calm that one would associate with someone psychotic. "I'm so fine that no one even saw this coming. I pulled Wechsler out of that apartment. I even asked him for so much flammable material so that I could use it to turn this place into a firetrap."

"Oh my god, you idiot," Alice snarled. "John handed that stuff over to you because he knew you'd use it!"

"So?"

"So he's using you to destroy evidence of what we've created here, and in the process creating a scapegoat for the coming war that will be too dead to defend herself."

"I'm hoping that scapegoat ends up being you," Alix muttered.

"Watch your mouth."

"Can't help it. It's in my DNA."

"Ha ha smartas-"

"WILL. YOU. BOTH. STOP. TALKING?!" Alison screamed. "I'm trying to purge the world of our disease, and you're making it very hard to motive rant!" She waved the detonator a bit too close to Alice, and the older woman lunged for it. Alison practically dove out of the way then kicked Alice in the face. "Fine then," she said. "I guess the explanations are over."

Before Alix or Alice could do anything, Alison hit the button, and their world went up in flames.

The control system in the Heroics base began to beep with alerts so loudly that Cass, on the third floor, could tell that it was going off regardless of the incessantly flashing light on her wrist. She bolted towards the elevator, but before she got there, a young woman appeared in front of her. Cass skidded to a stop, just barely coming to a halt before slamming into the other woman.

"Jeez! Sorry, Clarice, I wasn't expecting you. I guess whatever's going on out there is bad enough that the Alumni is responding to it, too?"

"Actually, the Alumni isn't going to respond to that alert," Clarice said emotionlessly.

Cass hesitated. "Wait, weren't you one of the heroes that disappeared? It was right around the same time Jetstream was taken." Cass glanced down at Clarice's wrists, but there was no band

149

there. She took a cautious step backwards. "What's going on?"

Clarice laughed. "You always were too smart for your own good, Cass."

"Haven't shown much of that recently, so I'm glad that you seem to think that it's coming back," Cass replied dryly. "What do you want?"

"How do you know that I didn't just escape?"

"Because nobody escapes," Cass said bluntly.

"You did."

It was Cass's turn to laugh. "Not really, and even if you think that I did, we've seen how well that went for me. Now why don't you tell me why you're really here, Porter?"

Clarice smiled. "Like I said, Cass. Too smart for your own good." A man in a Wechsler Industries security uniform stepped out from behind the elevator. "Wait here with Garrison for the other woman. Cabot. Then bring her to Wechsler," she ordered him. When he nodded, she gripped Cass's arm tightly and disappeared with her.

Kate climbed the last rung of the ladder that went to the roof. She headed over to retrieve her bow and quiver, which she had stashed there in order to go down to the street to look for Alix. As she secured her quiver on her back, she looked down Main Street towards Fuego Village. Her blood went cold. There was a large crowd of people walking towards the center of town, and, from what she could tell, every single one of them had a thick silver band on one of their arms.

12

"You know, most fathers can just call their daughters if they want to talk," Cass said in a bored voice. She was sitting in Wechsler's office, handcuffed to a chair. "They usually don't need to kidnap them and chain them to pieces of furniture."

"Yes, well, I didn't think you'd come if I'd asked nicely," Wechsler said, sitting in front of her on his desk.

"No, probably not. I've made the executive decision to stop willingly visiting people who want me dead." She shot a sideways glance at Clarice, who was standing in the corner of the room. "Out of curiosity, what's with your new guard dog? I thought you hated people with powers."

Wechsler smiled. "We have a mutual agreement in place. Consider the Alumni to be sort of like my Heroics. Except my group is much more experienced and much more willing to kill. Isn't that right, Clarice?"

"Yep. We aim to please." Clarice smirked. "Speaking of killing, how are the controlled idiots doing?"

"Well, as far as I can tell, I think they just engaged the Heroics brats. Now, if you don't mind, Clarice, could you go and initiate the next part of the plan?"

Clarice nodded. "Of course." She disappeared.

"Ah, alone to talk. Isn't that such a lovely thing?"

"I'm going to have to go with 'no,' since you're the conversation partner."

Wechsler smiled thinly. "Your sarcasm won't last much longer."

"I'm sure. Y'know, when the others realize that I didn't check the alert, they're going to wonder what happened to me."

Wechsler seemed to ignore her. "Honestly, I don't know why I don't just shoot you now. It would keep you from getting away. But the last time I shot you, you somehow survived, so I'm going to wait and make sure that I can guarantee you die this time." He laughed. "And then, after you're dead, I think I'll kill your boyfriend out of spite."

Anger lit in Cass's eyes, and her hands tightened into fists. "If you touch him, I don't care if I have to *come back from the dead*, I will *kill* you," she said, quietly and dangerously.

"You really do care. How cute. Unfortunately that just makes me want to kill him more." Wechsler looked at his watch. "And even more unfortunate is the fact that I might not get to do it myself. I asked them to bring him to me, but you know, the help can be so poor these days."

Cass paled. "What did you do?"

"What makes you think I-"

"*What did you do?*"

Wechsler smirked. "Let's just say that while we're talking, and while your vigilante friends are dealing with the issue in the city, my Alumni group is taking over the Heroics mansion." His smile took on a cruel edge. "And then they're going to burn it down, along with anyone who's still in it."

Alix hurriedly typed commands into the computer in the Shade Security warehouse, coughing into her hand as smoke began to fill the room. It was one of her worst ideas in a while, but she had to know what was happening. Information on the control bands popped up on the screen, and she cursed under her breath as she read it. Alix grabbed the cylinder that she had gone for, and was about to leave, but another file caught her attention. She summoned a drive from a shadow, plugged it into the computer, and downloaded it. While the opportunity presented itself, she wasn't going to lose whatever it was that Alice had been seriously trying to hide.

Kate fired two arrows at the oncoming swarm, pinning one of the controlled heroes to a wall. "We've got company!" she yelled down to the others. She bit her lip. The crowd on Main Street had realized that something was wrong and was currently running in every direction, trying to get out of the street before the fighting started. The other Heroics kids were busy fighting to stay out of the way from the fleeing stampede, and they couldn't hear Kate's voice.

She turned when she saw a shadow out of the corner of her eye. Alix appeared, rolling onto the roof in a move that looked painful. Kate stared at her. "You know you're on fire, right?"

Alix paused, looking at the flames on the bottom of her cape. She slapped at the flame until it went out and then stood. She moved her left hand experimentally, and Kate could see that there was a small burn on the palm. "Eh, I had to get rid of this cloak anyway," she said calmly.

"How did you even…?" Kate shook her head quickly. "No, never mind, I'll ask later. We need your help now. That entire crowd is made up of controlled empowered people. Think you can get the bands off?"

Alix stared at her for a moment. "I'm sorry, Kate. I've just come from Alice's warehouse. I did a bit of research. They changed the release command on those bands. There *isn't* one anymore. Those people will run until they die, and they can't even talk anymore."

"Isn't there anything we can do?" Kate asked, sounding scared.

The other girl swallowed and shook her head slowly. "No. I'm sorry, Kate, but if any of us try to remove those bands, we'll all just end up dead. I don't know how to save them, Kate. We might not be able to."

"Well then what good are you?" Kate growled.

Alix tensed. "Something's wrong."

"No shit."

"Not what I mean. Last time I felt this sort of feeling through my shadows, Wechsler was trying to murder AJ."

Kate studied Alix for a moment. The girl was fidgeting uneasily, her face turned away as if she was looking at something that Kate couldn't see. "Go. We'll handle these guys. It's important to make sure that the crew at the base is safe, and you'll get there even faster than Jay."

Alix nodded. "Good luck." She disappeared into the shadows.

Kate looked down into the swarm and sighed. "Yeah. We're going to need a lot of that."

Alix appeared on the main floor of the mansion. "Casey? AJ? Niall? Anyone? Is everything okay?" She frowned when she noticed the screen of the conference room, cluttered with dozens of flashing red lights. "What the hel-" Something hit her hard in the back of the head, and she fell to the floor.

Casey got off the elevator on the basement floor. She frowned and looked around cautiously. The control system was having the technological equivalent of a panic attack, but no one seemed to have noticed. It was odd to her, because the rule was that there had to be at least one person around to use the system at all times. She headed towards the control room. When she stepped inside, she saw that there were hundreds of emergency calls pelting the police station, fire department, and ambulance depot.

"What on earth is going on?" Casey whispered.

"Mr. Wechsler is attacking the vigilantes, Ms. Cabot," a voice said from behind the system controls. A man with blue eyes and graying black hair in a Wechsler Industries uniform stepped out. "You've been asked to visit him to discuss some things."

"Sorry, but tell him that I'm unavailable," Casey replied, trying to hide her nervousness.

"Sarcasm-backed courage," the man commented. "I've seen a lot of that in my lifetime. It's something that Tess basically runs on."

"Tess… You mean Cass? Where is she? What have you done with her?" Casey demanded.

"Tess was called away to a meeting with her father."

"A meeting?" Casey laughed. "Yeah, right. More like an execution. He'll kill her."

"Shut up," a second voice snarled. A man tightly grabbed Casey's upper arm. "You're coming with us."

Casey frowned down at his hand. "What, is that supposed to be my weak point or something?" She turned quickly and kneed the guard holding her in the groin. When the guard dropped to his knees, she grabbed a nearby paperweight and hit him in the face with it. As he fell to the floor unconscious, Casey whirled around to face the other man, preparing to defend herself. He hadn't moved.

"Good, now that he's been dealt with…" The man leaned against the table as if nothing had happened. "My name is Gabriel Garrison. Why don't we have a chat?"

The Heroics team was severely outnumbered. Jay zipped in and out of the swarm of controlled empowered people, grabbing individuals at random as he went and delivering them to Ray, who was corralling them in cells made of electricity. "We can't keep this up for much longer," Ray said as Jay tossed the fifteenth hero to him. He looked tired, the strain from keeping so much electricity stable getting to him.

156

"Hang in there, Blackout," Jay said, putting a hand on his friend's shoulder. "We have a job to do."

"Yeah, you keep saying that, Clash, but I still don't know exactly what we're doing here."

"Trying not to kill these guys," Jay replied. "This isn't their fault."

"True, but I have to say this," Ray said quietly. "If we can't free them and we can't kill them, what are we supposed to do?"

"Just keep doing what you're doing, bud. Targeter will figure something out." Jay frowned up at Kate, who was firing trap arrows at people who were flying and crawling up the building towards her. "I hope so, at least."

Kate put a hand on the edge of the roof, taking a moment to catch her breath. She could hear the others asking for orders through her sunglasses, but she couldn't figure out what to tell them. "I'm sorry, guys," she said quietly. "I'm running out of ideas. I don't want to kill these people, because they don't want to attack us, but I don't know what to do."

"Kate, I'm sorry," Julian's voice said. "I'm sorry, but we might need to start hurting these guys."

"Okay. Prioritize based on the threat to others. We- augh!" Kate's words were cut off as the roof underneath her collapsed.

"Where is everyone?" Niall asked as he stepped into the base.

157

AJ entered behind him and looked around, his eyes narrow. "I don't know. I don't like this." He walked over to the control room. "Oh, this isn't good."

"What's wrong?" Niall followed him, frowning. He froze in the doorway. "Oh."

The computer screens were all shattered. A sword made of pink energy was stabbed through the box under the desk that ran them. The tower that stored information on the members of Heroics was sparking with green electricity, and the file cabinet full of papers was on fire.

"What... the hell," Niall said slowly.

"Get to Casey's lab."

"What?"

"Casey's lab. Now." AJ turned and bolted out, heading for the opposite side of the base.

Niall hurried after him. "What do we do? What happened in there?"

"What we do is alert the others. As for what happened, I have no idea."

"You're lying," Niall said.

"What?"

"You have an idea. I can see it on your face. You aren't sure, but you have a thought towards what happened in there."

"I've seen weapons and electricity like that before," AJ replied. "Used by members of the Alumni."

"The former Heroics guys?"

"Yes. Their leader was one of the heroes that disappeared before. No one's seen her since, and the team hasn't talked about the situation with anyone."

"Do you think they were all taken and are being controlled?" Niall asked.

"I'm... I'm not sure."

"What, you think they might have done that on purpose?"

"They were always sweet kids, but something hasn't been quite right with that group for a while. I don't know if they switched sides or if they're just being difficult, but something's wrong."

AJ skidded to a stop in front of Casey's lab. It was on fire. "... Well okay then. That plan needs to be amended."

"Good observations all around, AJ," a voice said from behind them.

AJ and Niall turned. Seven kids were standing in a semi-circle around them. The one in the middle who had spoken, a young woman with pink hair, stepped forward.

"Clarice," AJ said. He glanced down at the wrists of all of them. "Not being controlled. Okay. This kind of sucks."

Clarice gave a thin smile. "You want us to be controlled by John Wechsler?"

"No, but it's better than you doing all of this willingly."

"You're as smart as Cassidy."

AJ tensed. "What have you lot done to her?"

The young man with blond hair who had been in line next to Clarice stepped forward to stand with her. "She's with Wechsler. They needed to talk."

"I wouldn't worry about Cassidy's fate, though, doc," Clarice said. "You two are the ones who are really in trouble here."

159

"Why's that?" AJ asked softly.

"Because we're here to destroy this place, take you to Wechsler as one final bit of punishment for Cassidy, and kill everyone who remains here." Clarice's green gaze shifted to Niall. "Which apparently is only going to be you, boy."

"Boy? You can't be that much older than me."

Clarice frowned. "I'm twenty-six."

"Really? You look a lot younger than that. Must be the hair."

Clarice's eye twitched irritably. "If you're trying to annoy me, boy, it's not going to work."

"Seems to be working to me," AJ said, smiling slightly.

"It won't have the opportunity to work any further," Clarice said coldly. "Blackwing?"

The blond man next to her looked over. "Yes?"

"I need to go take care of the last part of Wechsler's plan. You have my permission to kill these two as slowly as possible. Wechsler might want AJ alive, but if we give him a painful death he might not mind. If you can manage it, leave him just barely alive so that we can at least mostly fulfill our promise to deliver him."

Blackwing nodded. "Yes, ma'am."

"Don't let me down," Clarice replied with a smirk. She disappeared.

Dick "Blackwing" Lance took a threatening step towards AJ and Niall. Behind him, Kyle "Legion" Ichiki drew a pink energy sword out of thin air. Rahne "Shift" Garfield turned into a wolf. Bobby "Cryo" Munroe's fist turned to ice. Sofia

160

"Airwave" Munroe's hands started to spark with green electricity. Johnny "Spitfire" Aller's hands lit on fire. Dick smiled cruelly. "You two should probably run."

Kate opened her eyes slowly. The chunk of roof that she had been standing on was floating in thin air and was slowly rising back up into place. Kate looked up. Zach Carter was standing in between two other people- a black-haired woman, who was holding out a hand and seemed to be lifting the piece of roof up with telekinesis, and a brown-haired man.

"Try not to get yourself killed there, Targeter," Zach said, holding out a hand and helping Kate back onto the solid section of the rooftop.

"I keep trying my best, Kov, but this isn't exactly easy."

The brown-haired man held out Kate's sunglasses, which had been knocked off of her in the collapse. "Here. These are yours."

"Thanks," Kate said as she took the glasses from him and put them on. He was giving her a curious look, but Kate turned her attention to Zach. "What are you doing here?"

"This city is under the protection of the Security Legion too, remember?" Zach grinned. "This isn't just *your* fight, kiddo." He nodded at the woman. "This is Teleka." He nodded at the man, who was still studying Kate. "And this is Flare."

Kate gave a short nod. "Thanks for your help."

"Not a problem," Teleka said. "We're all heroes here."

"The issue here is that they're heroes, too," Kate said quietly, looking down at the fight, which was continuing below with some assistance from a few members of the Legion. She looked at Zach. "They can't stop themselves from attacking us. You know that."

Zach's jaw tensed. "Yes, we do know that. But we still need to take them out." He sighed. "We can apologize later... if any of them survive."

"That's a happy thought," Kate muttered.

"I know, Targeter, but we have no choice." Zach walked over to the edge of the roof to stand next to her and lowered his voice. "We have to do this, Kate," he murmured. "We have to."

"I know." Kate turned on her communications device. "Guys, listen up. The Legion is going to be joining us in the fighting. The plan is to take those controlled people down, even if we have to start hurting them. The safety of this city and the people living here is what's most important." She took in a slow breath. "Take them all out."

The order came through the sunglasses just as Lori threw two attackers back with a well-placed blast of water from a nearby fountain. "Good, because this was starting to get ridiculous."

"Starting?" Julian laughed. "I'd hate to see what fully ridiculous looks like through your eyes."

"It takes a lot for me to get to that point. I can control water with my mind, after all. If I call something ridiculous, it has to *really* be."

162

"Sounds logical enough to me." Julian used telekinesis to throw back three charging people. "How many of these guys *are* there?"

Kara landed next to him, looking out of breath. "From the looks of things we've knocked out or otherwise disabled about half of the crowd that was swarming here."

"Only half?" Julian asked weakly. He sighed. "This is going to be a really, really long day, isn't it?"

AJ and Niall bolted up the steps, taking two at a time. They burst onto the first floor of the Heroics mansion and headed for the emergency alert system that was hidden in the living room. AJ turned a corner quickly and tripped over the motionless form of Alix. He crouched down next to her immediately. "Alix? Alix!"

The girl was curled up in a fetal position, shivering with pain. Her teeth were gritted and her hands were clenched into fists. A gray band was covering her eyes, pulsating on and off with a white light. Every time there was a pulse, Alix flinched horribly.

"What is that?" Niall asked quietly.

"Some sort of device that seems to be blasting light into her eyes." AJ touched the band cautiously, and found that it wouldn't budge.

"Light like that hurts her, right?"

AJ nodded. "Poor kid's completely immobilized. That's the downside of having that kind of weakness."

Niall glanced behind him as he heard the sound of paws running up the steps. "Shift is coming. We need to go. We can move her, right?"

"We have no other choice."

Wechsler gave Cass a solid punch to the face, dazing her. "Do you know what I'm going to do to you, girl?"

Cass shook her head to clear it and then sighed. "No, but I'm sure you'll tell me."

"I've gotten an update from Porter. As soon as her people are finished having some fun with the good doctor, she's going to bring him here. I am going to make you watch while I kill him slowly and in the most painful way possible. I am going to make sure that you think long and hard about the fact that his death will be *your fault*, because I wouldn't have cared this much about killing him if it wasn't for the fact that I can see on your face how much you care about him. Then I'm going to take all of that emotional pain and add to it with as much physical pain as I can possibly put you through. And then I'll kill you."

Cass looked both furious and scared, but she kept her voice calm as she said, "You really, really do hate me, don't you? Why are you this determined to make my death hell? It's not your style. You either shoot people or use them in experiments until they die. This kind of aggression isn't your thing."

"It is when I'm really pissed off," Wechsler replied.

"Again, what the hell did I do to you?"

"You embarrass me." Wechsler started pacing in front of her. "I thought that I had a loyal soldier who also happened to be a very good test dummy." He gave her a disgusted look. "Instead I got a worthless traitor who not only abandons me to work for the enemy, but *falls in love with one of them*!" He stopped in front of her and put his hands in his pockets. "So I've decided to redeem you by making you part of a brand new experiment. I was going to test it out on your boyfriend, but now I realize that it would be so much more fun to do it to you."

"And what is this mystery experiment? How many people you can murder before the police arrest you?"

Wechsler smiled. "No. The experiment is how much pain a single person can take before they simply give up on living and die. And if you don't mind me saying, Tess... I do hope the amount of pain ends up being *very, very high*."

AJ and Niall were about the pick up Alix when a cage made out of pink energy formed around them. Kyle stepped in front of the cage. "Gotcha," he said with a grin.

Rahne jogged up behind him, back in human form. "Awesome job, Legion. Now let's take them back downstairs. Blackwing wants them." She took a step towards the cage, smirking. "You know, if someone trying to kill you gives you the chance to run, either keep running or head directly for an exit. You might actually be able to last more than thirty seconds."

"I'll keep that in mind for next time," AJ said, sounding annoyed and frustrated.

"There won't be a next time, doc. Definitely not for you, at least. Once Blackwing is done with you, you're being shipped off to Wechsler."

"You keep saying that, but so far no one's told me what he wants me for. I mean, he wants me dead, I'm aware of that, but why won't he let you just kill me?"

"Uh... AJ... Why are you asking them to kill you?" Niall asked in a murmur.

"Shh," AJ said to him, keeping his gaze on Rahne.

"It's simple, really," the woman said with a smile. "Wechsler wants to kill you in front of Cassidy before he kills her."

AJ fixed his tie. "I see," he said slowly, anger in his voice. "I really hate that man."

"The feeling is apparently mutual. Now come on. The longer this takes, the more chance we have of being interrupted."

AJ, Alix, and Niall were brought back down to the basement. Dick had stolen a chair from one of the rooms and was sitting in front of the elevator. He grinned at them. "That was fast. And here I thought your survival instincts were a bit better." He glanced at Alix. "Ah. You stopped to help the clone."

"You say that like we shouldn't have," AJ said quietly.

"Well, I don't really care either way," Dick replied, "but you probably could've at least gotten away if you hadn't bothered."

"What did you guys put on her?" Niall asked angrily. He was kneeling next to Alix, a hand on her shoulder as she continued shivering. Kyle had had to use an energy construct to move her down to the basement. At no point since Niall and AJ had found her had she shown any sign of being aware of her surroundings.

"Just a little creation of Alice's," Sofia said. "When she realized that Alix was going to be a problem, she made this. It's almost impossible to get off, and blasts the perfect level of light into Alix's eyes to keep her from doing anything. She can't even think straight enough to be able to talk."

"Why would you do something like that?"

Sofia looked at AJ. "Because she's too dangerous. She can escape too easily, and if she wants to go on offense, she has an advantage because her ability and talent with turning into shadow means that she can be defensive and avoid attacks while she's attacking. It's too good of a combination." She smiled slightly. "In a sense, she'd break the game."

"This isn't a game," AJ said, his eyes dark.

"No, but that's the best way to describe the reason for why we had to make sure that she was taken out first." Sofia shrugged. "This is how it works now, AJ. We are at war."

AJ shook his head, confused. "What war?"

"Wechsler wants to rid the world of vigilantes. That's why he's making them all kill each other."

"What?" AJ asked in a horrified whisper.

"The empowered people that he's been taking from Caotico City and the surrounding
167

areas? He put modified control bands on all of them. The bands can't be removed, and they all have orders to kill every vigilante that they come across," Rahne answered.

"I don't understand." Niall's hands were clenched into fists, worry in his eyes. "I don't understand why you'd be helping him. You're vigilantes, too."

Dick's eyes narrowed and went cold. "Our parents were vigilantes. They died furthering Wechsler's plans. They accomplished nothing, so they were of no help. We only have powers because of our parents' blood, and only used those powers because of what Stephanie coerced us into doing. Wechsler showed Clarice and me the truth. He showed us what we had become, and he showed us how to change ourselves for the better. Clarice and I know that following him is what is best for our team. Regular vigilantes are too dangerous to be kept alive." He got up from his chair. "Now, the two of you might not be vigilantes yourselves, but you heal them. Coordinate them. You're just as bad as them. Which is why you, and this base, need to be destroyed." He glanced at the fire that was still burning slowly inside Casey's lab. "Spitfire, are you still keeping that blaze contained to that room?"

Johnny nodded. Dick smiled. "Good. Leave it like that until I tell you otherwise." He walked over and grabbed Niall by the front of his shirt, dragging him away from AJ and Alix.

AJ took a step forward, but he was shoved back by Rahne. "Stay back, doc," she growled. "Don't worry. Your turn will get here soon."

"What are you going to do with him?" AJ demanded.

"I'm not quite as bloodthirsty as Porter," Dick replied, "so I'm going to make his death quick." He forced Niall to his knees and pulled a handgun out from behind his back. He rested it against Niall's forehead. "Stay still. If you do, this probably won't hurt."

13

Wechsler opened up his desk drawer and took out a handgun. He waved it in front of him, showing it to Cass. "Remember this? Your old friend?"

"How could I forget?"

"I never will understand how you survived that shot," Wechsler commented as he walked back around to the front of his desk.

"I don't know, either. And that's the truth." Cass shrugged. "I woke up in the hospital. I have no idea how I got there."

"I should've done a headshot." Wechsler shrugged as well. "Next time." He fished a key out of his pocket and tossed it to Cass. "Take the cuffs off of the chair and then put them fully on your wrists."

Cass studied the key for a moment. "And if I don't?"

"If you don't, bad things happen. I'll let your imagination figure out what kind of bad things."

Cass slowly uncuffed herself from the chair and then secured the cuffs on her wrists. "Happy now?" she grumbled.

"Very. Keys please."

She threw the keys at him. He put them back in his pocket and then hit a button on his desk. The wall to Cass's right slid up into the ceiling, revealing another room. Wechsler nodded at it, his gun tight in his grip. "Walk with me."

"Well sure, since you've asked so nicely." Cass stood up, glaring at him, and walked into the room. As soon as she took one step inside, she paled. "Oh my god. This is… This is…"

"It's not the exact same one," Wechsler said happily as he followed her inside. "It just looks exactly the same. We figured that if it worked before, why change it?"

Cass gripped the bridge of her nose, looking like she had suddenly acquired a headache. "This is the same setup as the lab that you…" She swallowed, looking a combination of uncomfortable and terrified. "The lab that you tortured me in," she finished quietly.

"I didn't *torture* you," Wechsler protested.

"You injected me with chemical mixtures that you knew nothing about and which caused unknown effects. Most of them did nothing but be extremely painful. The only time that I actually asked you not to, the *only* time that I actually begged you to stop, you strapped me down, performed the experiment anyway, and refused to give me any pain medication for four days. When my body finally gave up and I passed out, you woke me back up so that I wouldn't 'sleep through your point'," Cass retorted coldly. She turned and looked at him, hate burning in her gaze. "So yeah, Dad, I think that what you did to me qualifies as torture."

Wechsler swung out, striking her with his gun in the face so hard that it caused a gash on her cheek, which immediately started bleeding. "Don't talk back to me," he snarled.

Cass gave a humorless laugh. "I think that after all these years, I've earned my right to a little back talk."

"The problem with that logic, dear daughter, is that I don't agree. And seeing as I'm the parent, I reserve the right to punish any child who talks back."

Dick was about to pull the trigger of the gun pressed to Niall's head when a green arrow smacked into the weapon, knocking it out of Dick's hands and making it slid across the floor, the arrow embedded in its side.

"Sorry, but he's my sister's boyfriend. Normally I'd be inclined to let him get hurt, but since she loves him, I can't let you kill him." Justin was crouched in the doorway to the stairwell, an arrow aimed directly at Dick's chest.

"Justin, you have fantastic timing," AJ said with a small, relieved sigh.

"I do, don't I?" Justin grinned. "I was coming back to talk, but when the elevators weren't working I figured that something was probably wrong. So I grabbed my spare bow and arrows from my room before I came down here."

"Good boy." While the Alumni were distracted, AJ grabbed Niall's sleeve and pulled him back close to Alix. "Though you probably should've gotten some help first."

"Eh, I can handle these idiots," Justin replied, glaring around the room at the members of the Alumni.

Dick laughed. "What can you do? Your power is accuracy. You might as well be trying to talk us to death."

"You're one to talk. Your power is enhanced reflexes."

The other blond man gave Justin a cold smile. "You seem to be forgetting my other ability."

Justin frowned. Then, after a moment, his eyes widened. "Oh, crap," he muttered.

Dick opened his mouth, and a loud, piercing screech accompanied by a rippling wave of sound and force came from him. Justin dodged out of the way of the attack at the last second, just barely getting out of the path of the wave as it crumpled the door and threw it off of its hinges.

"You know, Dick," Justin grumbled as he quickly stumbled back onto his feet. "I've never met someone whose name perfectly represented who they are."

"Smart talk won't get you very far," Dick replied. "Let's see how well your accuracy does at close range." He hurried forward.

Justin shot another arrow, but Dick dodged out of the way. The arrow came uncomfortably close to AJ, but he moved aside just in time. Before Justin could load another arrow, Dick was there, knocking the bow out of his hand. It skidded across the floor, coming to a stop far out of Justin's reach. Dick took a swing at Justin's head, and the two quickly ended up in a fistfight.

The two men seemed evenly matched. Every hit of Dick's that made contact was followed up by an equally accurate punch from Justin. Justin lunged to the side as Dick used the scream again, and slashed at the older boy with an arrow that he pulled out of the quiver on his back. It ripped the front of Dick's shirt and gave him a gash, but didn't do enough damage to give Justin any ground. Dick kicked the arrow aside, breaking it in the process. Justin grabbed Dick's shoulder and brought his leg up, kneeing Dick in the gut hard. Dick doubled over in pain, but it only stopped him for a moment. He regained himself almost immediately, giving Justin a right uppercut to the jaw.

The Alumni started to seem to be gaining the upper hand when Clarice appeared and forced them apart. "Enough."

Dick took a step back, wiping a line of blood off of his mouth. "Why, Porter? What's up?"

"The fight in Caotico is taking a bad turn. One of the Heroics kids is down, but they've teamed up with the Security Legion, so they're starting to gain too much ground. We have a fight to crash."

Niall, Justin, and AJ exchanged scared glances, the word 'down' worrying them, but none of them said anything. Clarice looked at AJ. "The question now, doc, is whether it's worth taking the time to bring you to Wechsler."

"That's up to you, I suppose," AJ said quietly.

Clarice considered her options briefly. "You know what? Forget Wechsler. This used to be my home, so this is my call, not his. It's just as easy to let you die here. Anything you'd like to say?"

AJ smiled humorlessly. "I just have a question. You're the one who took Cass, I'm guessing? You never said."

174

"Yes, I am," she replied.

"I figured." AJ stared at her for a long moment. "Allow me to make one thing clear. Being a former member of Heroics won't help you. If anything happens to her, I will kill you."

"I'd like to see you try when you're dead." Clarice looked at Johnny. "Light it up."

Johnny nodded, and suddenly the fire that had been quietly burning in Casey's lab exploded, surrounding them all. Clarice grinned at AJ. "Goodbye, doc." She and all of the Alumni crew vanished, leaving AJ, Justin, Niall, and Alix in the middle of the inferno.

Julian gave a suppressed yelp of pain as a boulder slammed into the right side of his body. He felt his shoulder pop out of its socket as the force of the blow knocked him to the ground. He could only lie there for a second, pain making his vision blurry.

Lori threw two men away from her with two quick jets of water, and was almost immediately blindsided by a fierce attack from a woman who was carrying swords that seemed to be made out of diamond and were extending out of her hands. She was a hero that Lori knew from the Security Legion, a powerful woman who went by Adamas. Lori stumbled away from her, blood dripping into her eye from a deep cut on her temple.

Kara and Jay were being pushed into a corner, trying to push back an advancing crowd alongside two adult heroes. Jay was fighting with one hand, his other tightly gripped on Kara's shoulder to support himself. He couldn't stand up straight, the pain from several fractured ribs making too much movement impossible.

Kate turned her face away a little too slowly as an explosion ripped through the corner of the rooftop she had relocated to. Debris smacked her in the face, throwing her backwards onto the roof with a painful *thud*. She opened her eyes slowly, her head pounding. She could feel blood pouring out of a gash on her cheek and from her nose, which from her current guess was broken. She pushed herself up and crawled over to the roof's edge to look down at the state of the battle. Kate noticed something to her left, and her eyes widened. "NO!" she screamed.

Ray and Zach flinched as a blast of fire flew over their heads. "This is decidedly not fun," Ray commented as he shocked a woman who was sprinting towards him with claws extended from her fingers.

"Definitely not," Zach agreed as he held out a hand, moving a metal light post so that it smacked into a man who was dropping down towards them from above.

"Did you hear that?" Ray asked suddenly, frowning.

"Hear what?"

"It sounded like Kate screaming."

And there she was, having just rappelled down from a nearby rooftop. She was running, her face covered in blood. Though she seemed to be heading towards them, her eyes were looking at something past them. Ray and Zach followed her gaze and froze, horrified shock spreading through both of them.

Lori jumped backwards, trying to deflect Adamas's swings. She could see a mix of terror and apology in the woman's eyes, and suddenly Lori realized what was happening. Neither one of them could get out of this.

Kate had apparently recognized the danger as well, and was sprinting towards them. Lori could see Adamas note that Kate was coming, and the band forced her to prepare to spin at the exact right time.

Adamas gave Lori a pleading look. Lori nodded. "You realize you'll die, right?" The pleading look turned to one of acceptance. "At least give me something more solid," Lori said quietly. "I don't know... blink twice if you're okay with this."

The other hero, her gaze meeting Lori's, blinked twice. Lori sighed. "Okay." She lunged forward, grabbing the band on Adamas's wrist and pulling.

Both women staggered away from each other. The band on Adamas's wrist had begun to glow red. "I couldn't... stop," Adamas choked out. "I'm sorry." She collapsed to the ground, dead.

Lori fell to her knees, clutching at the wound in her chest that was bleeding profusely. At the last second, the band's survival instinct had kicked in, forcing Adamas to swing upward and plunge one of her swords into Lori's chest. Lori fell forward, only to be caught by a skidding Kate before she hit the ground.

"Lori! Lori, stay with me," Kate whispered, her voice cracking. "Lori, please!"

"The bands are different. They don't dose whoever tries to remove them," Lori murmured. She looked up at Kate. "I'm sorry. I had to try. Adamas and I both knew that as soon as we engaged each other, we were dead."

"You idiot," Kate cried. "Why would you do that? You could've run."

"No, I couldn't have," Lori choked out. "That's what we both realized. I was boxed in, and she could make her swords lengthen at any time. Even if I'd run, she would've just skewered me before I got two feet away, and if that had happened I would've died without being able to help her." Lori took in a shaky breath. The light in her eyes was fading. "At least this way only two of us had to die," she whispered a moment before she stopped breathing.

14

Cass hit the floor hard, coughing. If her estimate was accurate, she had at least two bruised ribs and maybe a third one fractured. Wechsler stood over her, a bored expression on his face. "And here I thought you were tougher than this," he commented.

Clarice appeared in the room. He walked over to her and held a quick, whispered conversation. Wechsler looked annoyed, but waved her away without yelling at her. She glanced once at Cass and then vanished. Wechsler headed back over to his daughter. "Update. Unfortunately, your boyfriend can't join us today. But that's okay, because he's currently in the process of dying." He smiled. "And your Heroics friends will all be dead shortly as well. You might as well give up and just ask to die, Tess. You've already lost."

"Sorry," Cass replied tightly as she slowly stood back up. "I'm not a big fan of dying."

Wechsler raised his gun, pointing it at Cass's head. "You'll die for good this time, kiddo."

"You keep telling me that, but, you know, it never actually happens." Cass moved quickly, pushing the gun aside so that it pointed at nothing, pulling him forward and bringing her knee up all in one fluid motion. When he doubled over she grabbed the cuff keys out of his pocket and ripped the gun out of his hand. She backed away from him, hurriedly unlocking and removing the handcuffs from her wrists. "You can thank Garrison for teaching me that one," she said coldly. She completely unloaded the gun and then tossed the bullets and the gun itself in opposite directions. "Your move, Dad."

A dark look formed on Wechsler's face. "If I were you," he said quietly as he started towards her, "I wouldn't get too cocky."

"Not to point out the obvious," Niall said dryly, crouching down to get away from the smoke, "but I think we're in trouble here."

"Brilliant deduction, Niall," AJ replied. He was examining the band on Alix's face closely, trying to find a way to remove it.

"Will you stop with her?" Justin grumbled. "We need to find a way out of here."

"She *is* our way out of here, you moron," AJ retorted. "If we get this thing off of her, she might be able to focus long enough to move us all." He frowned. "There's a line here where two pieces meet. If we forced something into it, we might be able to pry it open and damage it enough that we can get it off." He looked pointedly at Justin. "Something like an arrow."

"You want *me* to save *her*?" Justin asked incredulously.

"No, I want you to save *us*." AJ glared at him. "Which includes you, since that's the only person you ever seem to care about."

AJ and Justin stared at each other for a long moment. Then Justin crouched down next to Alix, pulling an arrow out of his quiver. He put the tip of it on the line and then pushed down, twisting as he went. The band cracked and then snapped, falling off of Alix's face. A thin gash near where the line had been was the only evidence that it had ever been there.

"Alix," AJ said urgently, shaking her by the shoulder lightly. "Alix, can you hear me?"

Alix blinked her eyes open, then shut them again quickly. "Ow," she muttered.

AJ gave a relieved sigh. "Good girl. Look, I know that you're probably still not in good shape, but I need you to get us out of here. The base is on fire, and we're stuck."

"What do you want?" Alix asked. She sounded groggy, the effect of the bright light obviously still present.

"Get us out of here before we all burn to death, please," AJ replied.

Alix nodded, her eyes still tightly shut. She looked like she was concentrating on something, and after a moment all four of them disappeared into the darkness.

Cass couldn't breathe. Losing the gun had seemingly only made Wechsler more determined to kill her, so in a fantastically brutal move, he had chosen to pin her to the floor and wrap his hands around her throat. Cass would have taken a moment to appreciate how John Wechsler- cool, calm, collected John Wechsler –was currently acting no better than a common murderer, but she was a bit busy choking to death.

Normally she had the upper hand in fights because of speed and skill, regardless of whether her opponent was a guy much heavier than her. But that was when she was standing up and could avoid things. She was helpless on the ground.

"You could've died quickly, with minimal pain. You're the one making this harder on yourself," Wechsler growled to her.

If she could've, she would've pointed out that he was the one making matters difficult, being the one doing the strangling, but she couldn't speak, and sarcasm probably wouldn't help much in the current situation anyway.

Cass looked around, trying to find something to push the odds back in her favor. She could see a very familiar silver object sticking out on the edge of the table next to her. It was the last thing she wanted to do, but she was running out of options. Frustrated and desperate, Cass swung out, hitting the table leg. The vibration knocked the object off of the table and onto the floor near her hand.

Wechsler, only seeing the swing, smirked. "Starting to lose it, dear?" He tightened his grip on her neck, and Cass realized that she truly had no choice.

She grabbed the silver band that had fallen from the table and brought it up, attaching it to Wechsler's wrist. As it made the familiar sound of attaching itself, Wechsler suddenly released his grip on Cass. She quickly scrambled away from him and stood.

Wechsler made a furious sound and started shivering. Cass backed away, looking startled and scared. Her father tried to push himself to his feet and failed, resorting to simply glaring up at her. "What did you do?" he snarled.

Guilt, fear, and sadness flooding through her, Cass stared at him. "I… I didn't…" she stammered. "I just expected it to make you stop." A look of realization formed on her face. "Your DNA. It wasn't set up to work with your…"

"I realize that," Wechsler spat. He wiped at his face as a line of blood began to drip from his mouth. "It was a rhetorical question." He pulled irritably at the band. "Get this thing off of me."

"I can't," Cass replied quietly. "Only Alice can, remember?" She gave a humorless laugh. "You've essentially screwed yourself over, Dad."

"If I die I'm taking you with me." Wechsler tried to get up again, but fell back down. His hands tightened into frustrated fists. "Even if I have to do it with my bare hands, I will *kill* you, girl!"

"I'm not going to come over to you so that you can," Cass replied. "So… I don't think that's going to happen."

Wechsler shot a garbled stream of curses at her and reached a hand weakly out towards his gun. Cass kicked it farther away from him and then turned away. "You're leaving me here?" he demanded.

"There's nothing anyone can do, and I don't exactly feel like I owe you anything." She crouched down in front of him, far enough away that he couldn't touch her. "I'm sorry. The sad thing is that I actually, truly am." She headed for the door and opened it.

Cass stopped dead when she stepped into the hallway and came face-to-face with a man in a security uniform who had graying black hair. She hesitated, swallowing nervously. "Garrison."

183

"Tess," Garrison said. "You should leave before the other guards get here."

"Not going to shoot me, Garrison?"

"... No, I'm not."

"... Why?"

"Because no matter what your father's said about you, I don't think you deserve it," he said softly. "Plus, it's my job to serve Wechsler. He never specified which one." The guard smiled gently.

Cass hesitated and then let out a slow breath. "Thank you."

"Any time, kiddo. Now get out of here before my less friendly compatriots show up and I *have* to shoot you."

Cass gave him a smile and then bolted down the hallway. Garrison watched her go for a minute and then walked into the room she'd come from. He looked impassively down at Wechsler. "Had a bad day, boss?"

"Garrison," Wechsler said in a tight voice. "Good. Help me."

The guard didn't move. "Why should I?"

Wechsler shot a death glare up at him. "You work for *me*, dammit, not my worthless bitch of a daughter!"

Garrison put his hands in his pockets and shook his head. "That's your problem right there, John. You never realized what she could be. She would've done anything for you. If you'd included her from the beginning, she probably would've worked for you and done whatever you wanted. She loved you, you bastard, and you threw it all away because you were too much of a coward to find test subjects that would fight back."

Wechsler coughed blood onto the floor and then growled, "So, what? You're going to let me die because I had a few failures as a father?"

"No, I'm letting you die because you deserve it. You taught me once that some people deserve death. I'm just following that logic." Garrison sat down on the table in front of Wechsler. "And since in about a minute I won't be able to say it to your face, I'll tell you now. I quit."

"Targeter, you need to move," Julian said, gently pulling at her arm with his good hand. His right arm was hanging uselessly at his side.

"Get off of me," Kate spat. She was still kneeling next to Lori, looking miserable.

"Kate, please," Julian whispered. He too looked close to tears, but he was holding himself together. "You're in charge, remember? We need your head in this."

"Just go away," Kate replied. "You take control."

"I can't. I'm terrible at it. That's why it's *your* job even though *I'm* the oldest, remember?"

"Shut up and do it, Ghost."

"But-"

"Go and make sure Kara and Jay are okay," Zach said, interrupting Julian as he and Ray walked over to them.

Julian looked at him for a moment before nodding and walking away. Ray glanced at Zach. When the older man nodded, Ray turned and followed Julian. Zach looked down at Kate.

"Targeter. We have a job to do." He crouched down. "I lost my best friend too, remember? Jetstream."

"Yeah, I remember," Kate said hollowly. "How can you possibly stand being here right now?"

"Because I have a responsibility here. Just like you do." He smiled slightly. "Plus, I owe Casey a favor."

Kate gave a quiet laugh and looked up at him, tears still tracking down her face. "I'm tired, Kov. I'm just so tired."

"Rest later." Zach stood up and held out a hand. "Rest later, or rest now forever. It's too dangerous out here to shut down."

Kate stared at his hand. After a moment, she took it and allowed him to help her to her feet. "Now what?" she asked.

"Now you take control of your team, and you end this fight." Zach grinned at her and then ran off towards one of his teammates who seemed to be having trouble with several flight-capable attackers. Kate started running towards the others, but a quick yell stopped her in her tracks.

"Targeter, watch your back!"

Kate turned around and flinched as a beam of energy headed straight for her face. Flare, who had called out to warn her, jumped in front of her out of nowhere and deflected the blow using fire generated from his hands. He turned to her. "Are you okay?"

"Yeah, I'm fine. Thanks, Flare," Kate replied. She hesitated. "You blocked that attack. It could've hit you."

Flare paused. "Well, you're my brother's girlfriend. I couldn't exactly let you get hurt on my watch."

Kate froze. "What?"

"I recognized your face." Flare lowered his voice. "You're Kate Oliver, right?"

"How... How did you...?"

"Like I said," Flare explained, lifting his mask up, "you're my brother's girlfriend."

"*Andrew*?" Kate exclaimed, shock spreading through her as she saw a familiar face under shaggy brown hair. "Andrew Sullivan? Niall's older brother?"

"The one and only."

"But... But how... Does Niall know that...?"

Flare lowered his mask again. "He doesn't know that I'm a hero, no. I didn't know how to tell him. I didn't know how he'd handle knowing that I have powers." He cocked his head to one side. "Does he know that you're a hero, too?"

"Yeah. He's been to our base and everything. We didn't know whether or not we could tell *you*. Niall was worried, because he said that your stepfather isn't too big a fan of heroes, and we didn't know whether you shared the sentiment. Apparently not."

"Apparently not," Andrew echoed, an amused tone in his voice. He gave her a mock salute. "We'll finish this conversation later. Right now we have a battle to win." His eyes showing that he was grinning beneath his mask, he turned and bolted towards Zach.

Cass hurried through the halls of the Wechsler building, periodically ducking into doorways to avoid being spotted by any members of Wechsler's security force. Garrison might have been their boss, but she was fairly certain that they wouldn't check in with him before they shot her. When she was little, Wechsler's security force had been made up of former soldiers who still had their senses of honor. The more corrupt Wechsler got, the more ruthless his soldiers got, until Garrison was the only good one left. From what Cass could tell, the only reason that Garrison was still around was because Wechsler needed at least one honest man to be in charge of the psychos.

Cass heard two guards start down the hallway that she was walking in. With nowhere else to go, Cass opened the door to her left and stepped inside a small room. She found herself inside a room full of monitors, all of which showed security camera footage that no one seemed to be keeping an eye on. For some reason, none of the screens were of the inside of the Wechsler building. Cass frowned, squinting at one of the monitors. A sudden memory flashed through her head as she recognized the place. And then, as if by fate, she recognized the person that suddenly walked into the view of the camera. "Dammit," Cass muttered as she checked that the hallway was clear and then continued her hurried path to the exit.

Casey's hands tightened in and out of fists as she stood inside of the electrified cage that had shot out of the floor as she had tried to escape Wechsler's lab.

"You know," a familiar voice said from behind her, "I didn't take you for one to repeat your mother's mistakes."

Casey turned quickly. "Cass!"

The younger woman was frowning at her. "You're usually smarter than this, Case."

"We'll discuss it later. Do you have any ideas on how to get me out of here?"

"One or two," Cass replied as she headed over to a nearby computer terminal. "Last I checked, these controlled the security systems. I should be able to turn the cell off."

Casey checked her watch apprehensively. "How long will it take?"

"I don't know. It could take a minute. It could take fifteen. It depends on how much the system has changed." Cass glanced back at her. "Why, do you have a busy schedule?"

"No. I just followed my mother's example a little *too* well."

Cass paused in the middle of her typing. "You... Tell me you didn't."

"I can't," Casey replied weakly.

Cass let out a low, slow sigh. "Oh, this is going to be fun." She continued typing, her pace a little bit more hurried than it had been moments earlier.

After about a minute, Casey started shifting anxiously. "Cass, just leave!" she begged. "I set this place to blow up; there's no point in both of us dying!"

"You're an idiot, you know that?" Cass said, still typing.

"So sorry that I thought that destroying a building full of mind control stuff was a bad idea. You know, the stuff sending out orders to those bands? It can't be reprogrammed, so I figured that destroying it was my next best bet. I'm an idiot for doing that?"

"That's not what I'm talking about," Cass replied as she squinted at the computer screen. "I approve of that. But you're an idiot if you think that I'm seriously going to leave you here to die. We're a team, remember?"

Casey laughed dryly. "I thought you were the one that usually forgot that."

"So did I."

"Cass, seriously…"

"Shut up, Casey!" Cass growled, quickly turning to face her. It was apparently a mistake, as she immediately gritted her teeth and doubled over with a pained expression on her face.

"Cass, what the hell? Are you okay?"

"I'm fine," Cass said, gripping the terminal tightly. She forced herself to stand straight again and continue working on the computer.

"You are certainly *not* fine. You turned around and it was like I punched you." Casey hesitated. "How did you know I was here, anyway?"

"Long story." Cass typed a few more commands, and the cage around Casey slid back into the floor. "I'll give you an abridged version when we aren't about to blow up. Can we go now, please?"

"Sounds like a plan," Casey said, and both women started running for the door.

190

Once outside and a safe distance away, heading back towards the mansion, Casey turned on Cass. "What did you do to yourself?"

"Nothing. I… I got into a little bit of a fight."

Casey frowned and narrowed her eyes. "For the love of god, Cass, there are bruises around your neck."

"Okay, so maybe it wasn't really a *little* fight. And maybe the fight was a bit more like a murder attempt. But I'm fine, really."

"Your father?" Casey asked quietly.

"… Yeah."

"How did you get away?"

Cass turned and looked at her with hollow eyes, and Casey gave a small, sad sigh. "I'm sorry, Cass."

"So am I. But you know, I'm not going to blame myself. He tried to kill me. More than once. I'm well over feeling guilt for the things that he's done."

"Good. Now why don't you tell me what almost made you collapse back there?"

Cass scoffed. "That would be the bruised ribs acting up."

"You really did get used as a punching bag, didn't you? I thought you were good at this."

"The strangling thing was because he outweighed me. The punching was because I was handcuffed."

"Handcuffed? Really? Coward."

"I do have to admit that it was probably a smart move for him."

"Not smart enough."

191

"How the hell did you end up in that lab, by the way?"

Casey paused. "There were two Wechsler security guards waiting for me at Heroics. I knocked one out, but the other didn't try to do anything. He said that he knew where the lab controlling the heroes was, and he asked me if I had a way to destroy the thing. I said that I did, and he got me into the building. He said that he couldn't guarantee that I'd be able to get past the security once inside, but it was the best he could do. So I gave it a shot."

"And almost got yourself killed doing it. Though I suppose I'm one to talk." Cass glanced at her. "This guard… Did he have a name?"

"I think he said it was Garrison."

Cass gave a small laugh. "Ah, Garrison. Figures."

Casey frowned. "You know him?"

Cass nodded. "He's the only adult in my life that I remember ever acting like I was an actual human being." She hesitated once before saying, "He was the one who told me to get out of the Wechsler building before the other guards got there. He knew that they'd shoot me on sight, either because they'd find it fun or because they'd probably know that I'd… that my father was dead."

Before Casey could reply, the two women came to a stop just outside of the front gate to the Heroics mansion. "Oh, god," Casey whispered. The base section of the mansion was on fire, and flames were licking up into the first floor. The top three floors looked unharmed, but the lower section was a lost cause.

"You know, when my father said that his team was killing AJ, I didn't expect him to be serious when he said that they were going to light the whole damn building on fire," Cass commented quietly.

Casey looked at her. "Killing AJ?"

Cass swallowed, looking scared and worried. "Yeah. Have I mentioned lately that my father hates me?"

15

Kate landed on her feet for a change, skidding backwards as a mountain of a man took huge swings at her. "This fight is never going to end, is it?" she asked breathlessly.

Zach laughed humorlessly. "Hey, don't complain. As long as it's still going, it hasn't ended because we lost."

There was a loud sound from the direction of Fuego Village, and suddenly all of the attackers froze. Sounds of shock and pain echoed all around the city streets as the controlled people- those who had been incapacitated as well as those who were still fighting –reacted to something. The man who had been attacking Kate and Zach collapsed onto the ground, and within seconds all of the remaining attackers followed suit.

"What's happening?" Kara asked as she walked over. She alone appeared relatively unhurt, with only a few cuts and bruises scattered over her face and neck. She was supporting Ray now, who was limping painfully. Jay was slowly walking behind her, and Julian was walking next to him, keeping an eye on him.

As if in answer to her question, the bands on all of the controlled people popped open and fell off.

"Well," Kate said, shocked. "Something went right for a change."

Zach looked around at the crowd of empowered people, all of whom were injured in some way and most of whom were very confused. He raised his watch up near his face and pressed a button. "Leader, this is Kov. We're going to need the Medical Corps down here. All of them. As soon as physically possible." He looked around at the Heroics kids and gave a tired, relieved smile. "I think you all can take a seat for a little bit now."

Cass and Casey made their way past the front gate of the Heroics mansion. As soon as they stepped onto the property, they heard a faint coughing sound to their right. They turned. Justin, Niall, Alix, and AJ were all on the ground, covered in soot and smoke. AJ was the first to his feet, coughing but otherwise seemingly okay. He looked up and saw Cass and Casey standing there, staring at them.

"Hey. Are you both okay?"

Casey nodded slowly. "We're good. You guys?"

"We're fine," Niall said through coughs.

Justin nodded in agreement, and added, "Alix is a bit out of it, but I think she's okay."

"Yeah, I'm fine," Alix said. She was lying on the ground, her eyes shut tightly. "I just can't see too well at the moment, but I'll be okay."

AJ frowned at Cass, who was just staring blankly at him. "Cass? What's wrong?"

Cass walked over to him and hugged him, a look of relief passing over her face. AJ hesitantly returned the hug, looking confused. "Are you all right?"

Casey walked past them and headed over to the kids as Cass shakily replied, "Yeah. Yeah, I am." Her voice was tight and strained, and the expression on her face was one of a person who had suddenly realized that there was something she had to say. As she gripped his back so tightly that her knuckles went white, she whispered something to him. AJ grinned widely before replying in a murmur that Casey couldn't hear.

Casey, who was pointedly pretending to ignore them, couldn't help but smile as she crouched down to put a spare set of sunglasses on Alix's face. Alix opened her eyes slowly. "Thanks," she said with a sigh. She glanced over at Cass, who was stepping out of the hug. "Did I miss something while I was concentrating on my pounding head?"

"Nothing really noteworthy, though I'm fairly certain that Cass just admitted that she loves AJ."

"Aw, dammit. Did you seriously win the secondary bet as well?"

"No, because Cass would have been the first to say it. Now hush before one of them hears you."

"That is in fact what I said, thank you, and it's too late. I already heard you," Cass said as she turned around. "Really, guys? Another bet?"

Justin shrugged. "Get rich or die broke."

Cass shook her head. "Well, who won this one?"

"I did," Niall said, holding out a hand to Alix and Casey. "I take cash and credit."

"We'll sort it out later. Once we know that the others are okay." Casey stood and helped Alix up.

As Casey went over to check on Niall, Alix walked over to Justin and held out a hand. Justin stared at it for a moment and then accepted it. Alix pulled him to his feet and said, "Thank you."

"For what?"

"For taking Alice's device off of me."

"I only did it so you could get us out of there," Justin replied grumpily.

"I believe that." Alix gave him a small smile and headed towards Cass and AJ. "Do we have any idea of where the others are?"

Cass shook her head. "They left after Wechsler had already sent the Alumni to grab me."

"That reminds me. How did you get here?"

Cass glanced at AJ. "I'll explain later."

Casey joined them with Niall. "I'm getting reports that there's a huge fight taking place in the middle of Caotico City, right around Monument Plaza."

"Then that's where I need to be," Justin said as he walked over.

"I can send you," Alix offered. "I don't think I should go, because I still can't see properly and wouldn't be much help."

Justin nodded. "Do it."

Alix held up a hand, and Justin dropped down into a shadow. Casey looked at the mansion. "We should probably do something about that."

"The fire system was getting ready to turn on when we left," Niall said. "The fire should go out pretty soon."

"Good. Then maybe once that thing starts working, we can get inside to see the damage. And maybe once we do that, we can figure out what's happening in the city."

"Targeter, what the hell happened here?"

Kate looked up as Clarice and the other members of the Alumni ran over to her. "Porter," she greeted quietly. She was seated on a curb in the middle of the chaos. The other members of Heroics had taken seats across the street, where they all looked exhausted. "Nice of you to show up."

"We were at the prison talking to a few of the empowered criminals that are locked up in there. When we got back outside we saw flashes of what looked like a fight coming from over here." Clarice looked around, a stunned look on her face. "What happened?" she asked again.

"The empowered people that Wechsler and Cage kidnapped were set on the city, being controlled by these band device things," Kate replied. She looked up at Clarice, her gaze dull. "They killed Torrent."

"I'm sorry," Clarice said.

Kate hesitated, frowning. She stared Clarice, her eyes narrowed. "Porter…" she said slowly.

"Yes?"

"Weren't you taken by Wechsler, too?"

The sympathetic look on Clarice's face vanished. "I knew that I shouldn't have gone with Wechsler's plan," she hissed softly. "I knew that pretending to disappear would only come back to bite me. It makes it so hard to play people."

Kate struggled to her feet, looking nervous. She started to back away from Clarice slowly, but found that, while she had been distracted by the conversation, the rest of the Alumni had spread out and circled her.

"What the hell?" Kate whispered. "What the *hell*?!"

"It's a long story," Clarice said. "I don't particularly want to get into it all over again."

"Long story short," Justin said as he stepped out of a nearby alley, bow in hand. "The Alumni here decided to side with Wechsler. And they tried to set me, AJ, and Niall on fire." He drew back his bow, aiming an arrow at Clarice. "And you know, that really pisses me off."

As the rest of Heroics quickly started getting up, realizing that something was wrong, Clarice glared at Justin. "You were supposed to die."

"Sorry. I have better things to do than follow your schedule."

Jay, Julian, Ray, and Kara formed a half circle around the Alumni. "What's going on?" Julian asked cautiously.

"The Alumni are here to kill us," Kate said.

"I never said that," Clarice replied, sounding hurt.

"Then why are you here?"

"To kill you. I just don't like assumptions."

Jay snorted. "You'll find that we're a lot harder to kill than you seem to think."

Clarice laughed. "Oh please." She looked around at the members of Heroics. "Out of all of you here, the only two who look completely able to stand are Pilot and Archer. And Archer doesn't even have a real power." She narrowed her eyes as her gaze rested on Kara. "Why don't we lower that number even more? Legion."

A thick pink band of energy formed around Kara, pinning her arms to her sides and squeezing her tightly. She was lifted up into the air as she struggled to free herself.

"What are you doing to her?" Kate demanded furiously.

Clarice shrugged. "Don't worry about it. You're all going to die anyway."

Kara was thrown backwards, slamming hard into the brick building behind her. There was a sickening cracking sound as something broke. She floated in midair for a bit, seemingly unconscious, and then she was thrown sideways into the small river that ran through the center of the city.

Kate moved towards Kyle but was held back by a quick burst of air from Sofia. "She'll drown," she said fiercely, glaring at Clarice.

"I'm pretty sure that's the point," Clarice commented.

Julian, recovering from the initial shock of the brutality of the action, moved towards the river. Before he could use his telekinesis to retrieve Kara, however, Dick jumped towards him and punched him in his bad shoulder. Julian yelled in pain and dropped to his knees, his good hand going up to grip his shoulder.

Clarice smirked at Kate. "Don't you see, Targeter? None of you are in any condition to beat us. And regardless, the only way to stop us is to kill us. Are you prepared to do that?"

"We're prepared to do whatever it takes to protect this city," Kate replied. "That's what we do. That's what we were raised to do. And if you had paid attention, you would know that that's what you were supposed to be doing, too."

"We *are* protecting this city. We're protecting this city from people with powers."

Kate held up her arms, gesturing at the destroyed city block that they were standing on. "Yeah, good job. Your protection obviously worked really well. You should be proud of yourselves."

"Every war requires some sacrifices," Dick said.

"Yes, and I'm sure that the people inside of these buildings, who are either injured or dead, really appreciate you sacrificing them for a cause that a good number of them probably don't even support." Kate shook her head slowly. "You're attempting genocide in the name of a man who has performed laboratory experiments on his own daughter. Do you really think that he's the kind of person that you want to be following? Do you seriously believe that he has everyone's best interests in mind? Seriously?"

"With moderate power comes moderate responsibility, and the arrogance associated with great responsibility," Clarice said dismissively. "What you're saying means nothing to me, Targeter. Now stop stalling. Either attack me or die like a coward."

Kate gave a desperate glance towards Zach. He and the other adult heroes were coordinating at the other end of the street. The only empowered people near the confrontation were either unconscious or dead. If she tried to yell for or otherwise indicate to Zach, the Alumni group would kill all of them before they could get any help. Their only options were to fight or die.

"Guys," she said slowly, "this is going to hurt like hell. But try not to die." She rapidly set an arrow in her bow, aimed, and fired it at Clarice.

The fight broke out immediately. Fueled by anger and their senses of self-preservation, the Heroics kids attacked the Alumni. Jay engaged Kyle, using his speed and endurance to fight off the pain from his fractured ribs. Julian used his telekinesis to offset the fact that he could only use one arm, and was dodging swipes from Rahne, who had transformed into a tiger. At the same time he mentally deflected blasts of electricity that Sofia was throwing at his back. Bobby and Johnny had teamed up as well, throwing ice and fire at Ray, who was leaning on his good leg and fighting back with his electricity. Justin was in a fistfight with Dick, who occasionally tried to use his sonic scream but for the most part relied on his physical skill. Kate was firing arrows at Clarice, who kept avoiding them by teleporting.

Kate pulled back her last arrow as Clarice appeared on her left. She released it just as Clarice vanished again. Kate lowered her bow slowly, looking horrified as the arrow she had aimed at Clarice embedded into Kyle's back. The man collapsed to the ground, but Kate had barely had time to realize what she had done before Clarice took advantage of her lack of arrows to appear in front of her and punch her, causing even more pain in her already-broken nose.

Kate's vision blurred with pain as Jay took a moment to check on Kyle and then hurried over to help Ray deal with the two Alumni members attacking him. Clarice reappeared behind her, but before Kate could turn, Clarice grabbed her shoulder and teleported both of them away.

AJ knelt down next to Alix, examining the burn on her left hand. The girl was still partially out of it from the blinding light, and she still couldn't see properly. Niall was crouched down on her other side, quietly watching AJ work. There was still shock in his eyes, and it was clear that he hadn't completely recovered from his near-death experience.

Cass, despite the bloody gash on her face and injuries to her ribs that were no doubt serious, had insisted that AJ find out if Alix was okay before he started to look at her. While he did so, Casey walked over to Cass, who was leaning against the wall that surrounded the Heroics property.

"Have you heard anything from the kids yet?" Cass asked quietly.

Casey shook her head. "No. Let's hope that it just means that they're busy."

The younger woman nodded slightly and then frowned as Casey smirked at her. "What?"

"I've never seen you that worried before."

Cass shifted uncomfortably, flushing just a tiny bit. "Yeah, so?"

"Nothing," Casey said. Though she was still smirking, a serious look formed in her eyes. "Don't hurt my brother, Cassidy."

"I don't plan to."

"Good. That's settled then." Casey turned to walk away, but before she could, Cass, smiling slightly, called her back.

"Hey, Casey?"

"Yeah?"

"Thanks. Thanks for not throwing me out of Heroics back then, even though your mother didn't want me there and you had no proof that you could trust me."

"Cass, generally I can tell whether I can trust someone. And I can tell when someone really, really just needs a friend or two." She grinned. "And besides, we'd be screwed if you hadn't switched sides. Who would tell those idiot kids where to go?"

Cass laughed. "I'm sure you could've handled it just as well as you already had." The smile on her face faded as she looked at the mansion. The fire had gone out, but they hadn't tried to journey inside yet. "Though I suppose that role doesn't really exist anymore."

"Oh, we'll be fine. Actually, I-" Casey stopped and turned as AJ started saying something loudly behind her. Alix was standing back up, an irritated and determined look on her face.

"Alix," AJ was saying urgently as he stood. "Alix, you can barely see and your head is still a bit screwed up. You said not long ago that you shouldn't go out there. You shouldn't even be *moving*, let alone fighting."

"I'm perfectly capable of going now that I've had a moment. I'm fine," Alix insisted.

"If I hear one more person who is clearly injured say that, I'm locking everyone in the med bay for a week," AJ said, sounding annoyed.

"Everyone else is out there, and for all we know *they're* hurt too! But they're still out there, so I'm going. I'll be back soon." Alix disappeared into darkness.

AJ gave a frustrated sigh. "I swear to god, that kid…"

"Lecture her later, AJ," Casey said as she walked over to him. "While she's gone, we should head into the mansion and see what happened in there."

"Well, it was on fire," AJ said dryly.

"I'm aware of that, smartass," Casey retorted. "I meant that we should see how bad the damage is." She started heading towards the building, Niall following closely behind her.

AJ looked at Cass. "Are you coming?"

"Yeah." Cass joined him and started walking with him. After a moment she reached over and took his hand. "How are you?"

"Not bad, all things considered. But I'm the one who should be asking *you* that," AJ said quietly. He glanced at the bruises on her neck but didn't say anything.

"I'm fine, AJ."

"Did you not hear my threat? Because I was quite serious about that, and-"

"I'm *fine*, AJ," Cass repeated. "Really, I am. It's been a very long day, and it's not over yet, so I just don't want to talk about it yet. Besides, I just want to know that *you're* okay."

"Me? You look like you got the crap beat out of you and you're worried about me?"

Cass raised an eyebrow at him. "Do I need to rewind today and go back to when I said that I loved you? Because really, you have to have forgotten if you're seriously asking me that question."

205

AJ gave a quiet laugh. "Oh, I haven't forgotten. I just… You should worry about yourself once in a while."

"Nah," she said with a smile. "It's much better to worry about someone else." She grinned. "Especially when the someone in question would totally get his ass kicked in a fight."

"Hey, I've seen enough movies to know that the medic and/or computer guy always ends up in trouble. I have taken the time to learn how to dodge."

"That's very impressive."

"I certainly like to think so."

They had just reached the front door of the mansion when Niall burst out of it, breathing heavily.

"Niall, what's wrong?" Cass asked, sounding concerned.

"The alert system… in the conference room," Niall panted. "It still works, and can still show what's happening in the city."

"And?" AJ prompted.

Niall looked up at him, his blue eyes wide with fear. "It's bad. It's really, really bad."

16

Zach turned, startled, when Alix suddenly appeared next to him. She was supporting a soaking wet Kara, who had an arm wrapped around Alix's shoulders and was hopping as she walked, putting no weight on her left leg.

"Pilot? Thief? What happened?"

"I think her leg is broken," Alix muttered as she helped Kara sit down.

"But how? She was fine a few minutes ago."

Kara looked up at him, her hazel eyes full of pain. She gave a weak laugh. "Have you looked behind you recently, Kov?"

Zach turned. At the opposite end of the street, just far enough away that the sounds hadn't been able to reach him, a battle was raging. He squinted. "Is that the Heroics kids fighting the Alumni?"

"Yeah," Kara confirmed. "That's old news." She gritted her chattering teeth. "I'd go over there and help, but this stupid leg hurts so much that I can't focus well enough to fly."

"I'll go." Alix stood up, just a tiny bit shakily. Zach couldn't see her eyes, and couldn't see any injuries, but from the tense way she was standing, he could tell that she was hurt too.

"I'll go, too," Zach said. He looked over at Teleka. "Can you give the rest of the orders? I have another fight to get to."

Teleka nodded. "Do you need some extra hands?"

Zach shook his head. "No. There are..." He squinted off into the distance again. "There are five enemies. I think we can handle ourselves." He tapped a finger on his watch. "If I need help, I'll call."

Teleka nodded again, and Zach stepped towards Alix. "Shall we take the fast route?"

"Sure, why not?" Alix looked down at Kara. "Try to relax, at least for a bit, okay? If you hurt yourself more, you'll be no use to any of us." She and Zach disappeared into darkness.

In the split second that it took for Alix and Zach to get to the fight, Rahne had been hit in the chest by a powerful blast of electricity. Sofia had knocked Julian to the ground, and Rahne had jumped at him with claws and teeth bared. In an instinctive move by Ray, he had thrown an attack at her just in time to save his friend. Julian scrambled backwards as a now-human Rahne fell to the ground, twitching. An accidental bit of aiming had led to Ray's attack hitting her right above the heart.

As Sofia, looking furious, threw an attack at Ray in retaliation, Zach and Alix appeared right between them. Zach immediately raised a metal manhole cover in front of him, using it as a shield to block the bolt of electricity. As Ray continued fighting Bobby and Johnny with Jay, Zach helped Julian to his feet. Alix moved forward to intercept Sofia, and the two started to fight.

"This is insane, Zach," Julian said breathlessly. "This is insane."

"I've gathered that," Zach replied sympathetically. He looked around. "Where's Kate?"

Julian shook his head. "I don't know. Porter disappeared with her somewhere."

Zach let out a slow breath. "Something tells me that's not good."

Kate blinked and suddenly found herself on the top of the Wechsler building. She was fine with heights normally, but this was way too much even for her. She stood incredibly still in the center of the roof, nervously looking around for Clarice. The woman appeared a few feet in front of her. "What's the matter, Targeter? I never pictured you for a fear of heights."

"I'm not afraid of heights," Kate replied. "I just have the natural human fear of plummeting to my death off of a skyscraper." She stared at Clarice. "Why did you bring me here?"

Clarice shrugged. "Because I could. That's the reason behind a lot of things, isn't it?" She smiled slightly. "Plus, it was getting a bit crowded down there. The clone girl showed up."

Kate frowned. "Alix?"

"Yes, her. I don't think anyone else noticed, but I saw her heading for the river when the fighting between our two groups started."

Kate swallowed, daring to feel relieved. "So Kara might be okay."

"Maybe. For now. She won't be once my team finishes with her regardless." Clarice's hands tightened into fists. "At the moment, you should be worrying about yourself."

"Why are you singling me out? I don't have powers."

"Well first of all, we're both the leaders. Second of all, yes, you don't have powers, and neither does your brother. But take a good look, Targeter. You have a broken nose. It's not hindering you too much. He doesn't have any injuries at all. The only two people in a team of heroes that have virtually no powers, and yet you're the two who got through a fight between dozens of empowered people essentially unscathed." Clarice started towards her. "And I want to know what it will take to kill you."

Justin jumped out of the way as Dick used his sonic scream in his direction. Out of the corner of his eye, he saw Sofia hit Alix in the side with a combined blast of wind and electricity. He kicked Dick in the face and then sent an arrow flying at Sofia. It hit her in the side of the neck, immediately putting her on the ground.

"SOFIA!" Bobby screamed from the other side of the street. He ran from the fight with Ray and Jay and skidded to the ground next to his fallen sister.

Justin stared at the crying man, looking stunned. While he was distracted, Dick kicked his legs out from under him, knocking him off of his feet. Justin slammed into the concrete, his bow slipping from his grip. He reached out to pick it back up, but before he could touch it, Dick's boot stomped down on his outstretched hand. Justin yelled out in pain and immediately pulled his hand back. Dick stared down at him, his hazel eyes cold.

He reached down and picked up one of Justin's arrows. He raised is up, preparing to stab Justin with it, but as he started to move his arm downwards, one of Kate's discarded arrows stabbed through his chest.

Dick dropped the arrow he had been holding and stumbled backwards. Alix moved out of his way as he went and stood next to Justin.

"Why... Why would *you* protect *him*?" Dick asked, his voice weak.

"Because it's what I'm supposed to do," Alix replied quietly. "I'm a member of Heroics just like he is." She shrugged. "Besides, he protected me, too."

Dick fell onto his back, struggling to breathe. He looked over at Bobby, who was kneeling next to Sofia. "Cryo," he choked. "Cryo, help me."

When Bobby didn't move, Dick's eyes gained a furious glint. "*She's already dead, dammit*! You can still help me! Leave her, and get over here!"

"You're a cold-hearted son of a bitch, aren't you?" Alix commented quietly.

"Seriously, Dick, she was your teammate," Justin muttered.

Dick ignored them. "*Cryo!*"

Bobby glared at him through his tears. "Just shut up, Blackwing," he said in a wavering voice. "Just shut up. You brought us into this and promised us that we'd be doing good things. You promised us that we were fighting the bad guys. That we would win because we were right. Does this look like winning to you?" He turned back away, staring at Sofia's body.

Johnny stopped his fight with Ray and Jay and walked over to Bobby, going right past Dick without saying a single word. He looked down at Bobby for a long moment, and then he knelt down next to him, silently putting an arm around his shoulders comfortingly.

"I think that's your answer, Dick," Alix said as she helped Justin to his feet. "Looks like you're dying alone."

Dick glared at her, but before he could respond blood started to drip from his mouth, and he took his last, shaky breath.

As Alix and Justin looked down at the second-in-command's body, Jay, Ray, Julian, and Zach walked over to them. Ray, who had been fighting despite his limp, was now using Zach's shoulder for support.

"I think this fight's over," Justin said quietly. He reached out to help Jay, who was now beginning to falter from the pain from his broken ribs.

"What about them?" Jay asked, nodding at Bobby and Johnny.

"Let them be," Julian said. "They aren't trying to fight us. So let's just let them be."

Justin glanced around. "Has anyone seen Kate? Did Porter take her somewhere?"

Zach nodded. "Yeah, but none of us knows where. No one's seen either of them since the beginning of the fight."

Justin swallowed, actually looking scared. "I have a bad feeling about this."

"Why not let yourself die, Targeter?" Clarice asked mockingly as Kate dodged out of the way of her fist.

"I really would prefer not to die today, thanks," Kate replied, flinching as a gust of wind pushed her sideways and almost caused her to get hit by another one of Clarice's punches.

Clarice frowned as Kate ducked under another blow and then swung upwards, making solid contact with Clarice's face. Clarice wiped away the line of blood dripping from her split lip. "It's all fun and games until your victim starts fighting back," Clarice said coldly. She reached behind her and produced a handgun from behind her back. "You know, Blackwing was going to kill your boyfriend with this gun. Your pain in the ass brother stopped him. Since the Thief is here, I'm presuming that your boy toy survived, but I'm actually quite saddened by that fact. I wish that I could tell you that he was dead before I killed you." Clarice cocked her head to one side. "Well, what do you know? Look at me. I'm thinking like Wechsler." She shrugged. "No matter. I'll succeed where he most likely failed."

As Clarice raised the gun, Kate held up her left hand. "One quick thing. Do you know why I have the name 'Targeter,' Clarice?"

"Because your power is accuracy. Yes, I know."

"Well, here's the thing. When someone with enhanced accuracy has full control over their powers, they can make some really tricky shots." Kate smiled slightly. "Even when it's extremely windy." Her miniature crossbow dropped into her right hand. She raised it and fired once, just as Clarice fired the gun. The arrow hit the bullet in midair, knocking it aside before it embedded itself into the barrel of Clarice's gun.

Clarice pulled the trigger again, but the gun wouldn't fire with the arrow inside of it. She looked up at Kate, stunned. "That's not possible."

"Normally you would be right, Clarice." Kate smirked. "But that's the funny thing about having a 'useless' power. Sometimes it comes in handy." Kate braced herself as Clarice tried to pull the trigger again. "And now that you've tried twice to fire a bullet past my arrow, you've probably irritated it enough for it to go off."

"For what to go off?" Clarice asked, confused.

"Stephanie didn't use all of Casey's explosives."

A stunned look of realization appeared on Clarice's face as the gun exploded in her hands. Clarice dropped the gun quickly, yelling in pain at her burnt and broken hand. Kate hurried forward, pulling one of her crossbow bolts out. She tripped Clarice, sending her to the ground, and then stabbed the bolt through Clarice's arm until she was pinned down to the roof. "We all have weaknesses," Kate said breathlessly. "Every power has a downside." She gave a crazed laugh. "And yours? Yours is that you can only teleport when you can focus solely on your powers. Which means that if you're in pain, like from a crossbow bolt being in your arm, you can't do anything."

Clarice glared up at her. "What's your plan, Kate? Going to leave me here?"

"No," Kate said coldly, pulling out another bolt and loading it into her crossbow. "I'm going to kill you." She aimed the bow right at Clarice's throat.

"Kate, no!" Kara appeared on the roof, hovering an inch off of the ground so as to not put weight on her damaged leg. "You can't!"

"Why can't I?" Kate asked in a snarl. "She sided with Wechsler. She helped him cause all of this. And if all of this hadn't happened, Lori wouldn't be dead."

"I know, Kate, but you can't kill her," Kara said quietly.

"Why not? Why don't any of you care? Lori is dead! She was a sister to all of us! *Our sister*! And you're acting like she was just a soldier!"

"Because she *was* a soldier, Kate!" Kara said angrily. "We're *all* soldiers!" She finally lost the weak control of her powers and collapsed onto the roof, but she continued talking. "You heard what Stephanie said. You know how she manipulated us. When push comes to shove, all we ever were supposed to be was soldiers. But we come out here every day, and we help people. We know that we're risking our lives but we do it every day, because it's what we do. We *save* people. We don't kill them. That's not us. You really think that Lori would want you to kill Clarice out of petty revenge?"

"You think I'm petty?"

"*Listen to what I'm saying*," Kara said fiercely, obviously frustrated. "We're the good guys! We don't kill defenseless people just because we want to! Yeah, I want her dead, too, but I'm not going to kill her because Lori wouldn't want me to!"

Kate faltered, but continued on stubbornly. "Why does it seem like I'm the only one who's upset here?"

"You aren't," Kara insisted. "You really aren't, Kate, but the rest of us know that we have a job that we need to do. We can't break down. Not yet. We still need to keep a straight head. There's plenty of time to grieve, Kate, but it can't be now."

Kate paused. "You really are too smart for your age, Kara."

Kara smiled slightly. "Maybe I really am getting to be too much like you. Come on, Kate. Put the bow down. This isn't worth it."

After a moment, Kate said, "Fine." She lowered her crossbow and then kicked Clarice in the face, knocking her out. "What?" she said as Kara gave her a look. "Just because I'm not going to kill her doesn't mean that she doesn't deserve a boot to the face."

Kara shook her head slowly. "Yeah, fine, you're right."

Kate crouched down in front of the youngest member of Heroics and rested a hand on her cheek. "You're okay?" she asked quietly. "I thought they'd killed you."

"I'm okay. My leg is broken, and I only just managed to focus enough to get myself up here, but it doesn't really hurt all that much anymore. And I think I might be wet for weeks, but at least I'm not drowning."

"We seriously need to talk to someone about the safeness of having a river running through a city."

The younger girl laughed dryly. "What are they going to do, politely ask if it could change its course and start going around the city instead?"

Kate grinned, but the smile quickly faded as she looked down at Clarice. "What do we do with her?"

"Well, I can chuck her over the edge if you've changed your mind."

"I'm serious, Kara."

Kara shrugged. "I guess we send her to prison for the multitude of kidnappings and murders that she knew about and helped succeed. If you're okay with that."

The Heroics leader gave a scoffing laugh. "Pilot, I am more than okay with that."

17

Leaving Zach to deal with the three surviving members of the Alumni, as well as the cleanup of the battle, the Heroics kids traveled back to the mansion using Alix's shadows. Kate was one of the first ones to step out of the darkness and into the entryway of the mansion. She saw Cass and AJ sitting next to each other on the stairs, worried expressions on their faces and their fingers interlocked between them. Casey was staring at the monitor that flipped out from behind a picture, as Niall paced anxiously behind her.

It took a long moment for any of them, distracted by their thoughts, to realize that the Heroics kids were standing right in front of them. AJ looked up, blinked as the sudden recognition startled him, and then grinned. "Nice of you to finally show up."

At his words, Cass, Casey, and Niall all looked over. "Oh, thank god. You're all okay," Casey breathed. She narrowed her eyes as she surveyed the group. "Wait... where's Lori?"

Kate swallowed uncomfortably as a deafening silence answered her. The four base operatives stared at them for a long moment, and then realization seemed to strike all of them at the same time. AJ's grip on Cass's hand tightened, and she rested her forehead on his shoulder sadly. Niall looked down, his hands clenching into fists. Casey just paled, looking like she was trying very hard not to cry. "Oh," she whispered. "Not all okay."

Kate swallowed again. "We can grieve once we've had a moment to breathe. If it's all right with you, I just need to not think about it for a little while."

Casey nodded, still pale. "That's perfectly fine with me."

AJ was halfway through examining the Heroics kids when Kate walked over to Casey. "I forgot to ask. Are you guys okay?"

Casey nodded. "Yeah, we're okay. What exactly happened today?"

"The Alumni tried to kill us. We won. And we got a little bit of adult help, too."

"Oh, the grown-up heroes finally decided to acknowledge us outside of our own base? I bet you enjoyed that."

"They actually bothered to fight alongside us, yes, but I think they enjoyed the fact that they got to save us a bit more than we enjoyed being saved."

Casey smirked. "I bet they did."

"Kov says hi, by the way."

"Zach Carter? He showed up?"

"Yeah. He said that he owed you a favor."

Casey snorted. "Try several."

Kate gave a slight smile. "Yeah, he said that if you ever need him to pay up, just call him."

"Oh, trust me, I will."

"I'm sure."

Casey frowned. "What... what's with the smirk?"

"Nothing," Kate said, her smirk widening.

"There's nothing funny. I don't... you don't think that... Zach and I are not..."

"Whatever you say." Kate, her smirk breaking into a grin, started heading over to Niall.

"I'm not- Katherine Oliver!" Casey stared at her, slack-jawed.

Cass, who had been talking to an immobile Kara, wandered over to stand next to Casey. "I think this is karma."

"Shut up, Cass."

"I've earned the right to tease you, I think."

"If you have, then I'm allowed to tease you back," Casey pointed out.

Cass snorted and then winced as the sudden motion sent pain through her ribs. "You would anyway, so I might as well let myself throw punches of my own."

"Good point." Casey gave a slow sigh. "How do we recover from this, Cass? One teammate- one *family member* –dead, and the rest of them seriously injured, not to mention the deaths from before the battle. More betrayal than most people have to go through in a lifetime. Our base is destroyed, and we only barely avoided losing the place where we all live."

Cass smiled slightly. "We take punches and get back up. That's our job. That's what these kids do every day." She shrugged. "Will it be hard? Hell yes." She looked at Casey, her metal gray eyes clear. "But we'll do it anyway."

Casey gave a small nod. "Good. Because we'll have to."

Kate approached Niall slowly, almost shyly. "How are you?" she asked quietly.

"Not bad for almost being burned to death, though as you had a much rougher day than I did, I'm not going to complain." He just looked at her for a second, and then pulled her into a tight hug. "Don't do that to me again. Please just don't do that to me again."

"Do what?"

"Make me utterly terrified that you aren't going to survive."

His girlfriend gave a soft laugh. "Be careful, Sullivan, or people might start thinking you care."

"Good, because I do."

Kate hesitated. "I don't know if I can promise you that. With what I do, with what I am, I don't know if I can promise that I won't worry you again."

"Then do me one small favor," Niall said as he pulled back and looked into her eyes. "Always try your best to come back."

She smiled slightly and kissed him. "Always."

Niall grinned at her. He glanced over at AJ, and said, "We'll talk more later, but I want to see if AJ needs help. He, Casey, and I are the only ones that aren't hurt, so I might as well make myself useful."

"Good idea," Kate said with a smile as she watched him walk away.

While AJ was talking to Casey before the latter went to bed, Cass walked into the library and turned on the light. She jumped, startled, when she saw Alix sitting in one of the chairs and staring absentmindedly out the window. "Sorry, I… I didn't know you were in here," Cass said.

"It's okay," Alix replied. "Come on in. I'm just sitting here brooding."

Cass sat down in one of the chairs. She frowned slightly. Sitting on the table between them was a needle and an empty syringe. "Do we need to start sending you in for rehab, or have you not mentioned that you're diabetic?"

Alix didn't even smile. "It was a formula to slow down my aging."

"Trying to outlive all of us?"

Alix shook her head. "Just trying to live in general, really."

Cass studied her for a moment. "What do you mean?"

"I was created six years ago."

The older woman blinked. "You look like a teenager."

"Physically and mentally I'm nineteen. But my creation was only six years ago. Alice used an aging formula. It sped up the aging of me and Alison which, combined with false memories, allowed us to become full-fledged teenagers in the time it takes regular people to begin learning how to read."

"That's crazy, Alix."

"I know." She laughed dryly. "Come to think of it, putting that stuff in me was probably crazy too."

Cass glanced at the needle. "What was it for?"

"Alice created a counter to the formula she gave us in case she ever needed to adjust our aging back to that of a normal person. She wouldn't let us take it because she *wanted* us to burn out if we didn't die like all the others. When Alison set the place on fire, I knew that if I wanted to get it, I had to get it then. That's also when I found out about the adjustments to the control bands."

"I'm going to have to say that you probably should've have taken that, Alix. It's Alice Cage. She's not exactly someone whose word I would trust."

"I know that," Alix replied. "Trust me, I know, but what choice did I have, Cass? I could've either taken this formula, which might work, or let myself age three times as fast as everyone I know and care about. I'd rather take the risk."

"Okay. I'll accept that."

"Good."

Cass shifted. "So… How did your attempted murder go?"

The younger woman paused. "How did you know?"

"Well, given the way my day went…"

"Ah. Right." She sighed. "Alison tried to blow herself, Alice, and me up. I think the stress from finding out that she's a clone finally broke her. The later clones have a habit of being not entirely mentally stable."

"I'll have to keep an eye on you then."

Alix smiled slightly. "Yeah. I don't care much about Alice's fate, but Alison… I just feel bad that her entire life crashed around her so effortlessly. I was never her biggest fan, but it wasn't really her fault."

"I can certainly sympathize with that."

There was a pause as Alix looked steadily at Cass. "What about your father?"

Cass's jaw tensed. "I put one of the bands on him."

For a second the statement didn't seem to click in Alix's head, but then her eyes widened. "Oh. I'm sorry."

"I am, too. But he had his hands around my throat. I…"

"Didn't have any other options," Alix finished softly.

"Yeah." After a long moment, Cass said, "Alix… Can I ask you something?"

Alix looked wary. "I suppose."

"If you have unadulterated memories of the previous clones, then-"

"Cass, I can't tell you anything past what I already have."

Cass hesitated. "Why not?"

"You don't deserve to know the things that I know, my friend."

"Deserve?"

"Not in the bad way," Alix clarified quickly. "Most of the stuff that I refuse to tell you guys I'm hiding to protect you. There are some things that are better not knowing, Cass."

"What gives you the right to decide that?"

Alix smiled sadly. "Consider it a curse that I don't feel like sharing."

"Sometimes I think you know too much about too much, Al. Like how you were the one who took me to the hospital when I was shot. Casey told me. You keep showing up and saving our lives, but you still don't trust us enough to tell us things that are important, at least to us."

Alix paused a moment, looking conflicted. "Okay, I'll tell you *one* thing. *One*. And I'm only going to tell you because I think you should know it."

Cass looked a bit uneasy. "If you're already giving in to my request and breaking your own rules, it must be a pretty big thing."

"It is. And I'm not sure how you'll react to it."

"Well, come on then, Tolvaj, I don't have all day."

Alix hesitated again and then said, "You and AJ were a bit... more than friends when you were younger."

Cass stared blankly at her. "You mean... Are you saying that... AJ and I..."

"You were never officially together, no. But it was obvious to everyone that you'd started to crush on each other, hard. As far as I know, you only kissed once."

The other woman blinked. "As far as you know?"

"One of my past lives might have walked in on the two of you making out once," Alix replied slowly.

Cass, looking overwhelmed, stammered, "Wha- What happened?"

"Nothing. She walked out. You were both a bit preoccupied, and she certainly wasn't going to interrupt."

Cass flushed slightly. "You make it sound like we were-"

Alix gave a small smirk. "You were only kissing. But I will say that I'm not surprised that a little memory loss didn't get in the way of you two ending up together."

Her friend scoffed. "Were we really that obvious?"

Alix's smirk broadened into a smile. "Cass, you're so obviously in love with that man that it's ridiculous. Take a look around. You haven't gone to bed yet despite the terribly awful and tiring day that you've had because he's not there yet. Am I right?"

Cass blushed a bit more. "I don't know what you're talking about."

"I'm sure."

After a moment of fidgeting, Cass asked, "Why does everyone do that?"

"Do what?"

"Go out of their way to say how obvious AJ and I are. It's nonstop."

Alix shifted in her chair, studying her briefly. "Cass, I'm going to be honest here. You're broken. Not just broken, *shattered*. And even if the others didn't know the specifics, we all can see that much. We joke and we bring it up a lot in a weird way of encouraging you. Making sure that you see what you have. Because you can't be fixed, Cass. But that doesn't mean that you can't live."

"You don't need to worry about me," Cass said quietly.

The younger woman smiled slowly. "I don't think that's going to stop anytime soon."

Before Cass could reply, AJ walked into the room. "I'm going to bed," he said.

"Thanks for the announcement," Alix replied snarkily.

"Nobody asked you, Alix," AJ retorted.

"We're in a feisty mood today, aren't we?"

"No, we're just very tired and very much not looking forward to weeks of injured teenagers. No offense, but people your age complain a lot."

"Says the man who's complaining."

AJ started to say something, but Cass's short laugh cut him off. "Don't start fighting, you two," she said, getting to her feet. "I'm not about to deal with that this late at night." She walked over to AJ, grabbed him by his tie, pulled him forward, and kissed him deeply.

"What was that about?" he asked.

"Nothing special," Cass replied, shooting a glance at Alix. "Just... thinking about some new information."

AJ frowned. "New information?"

"I'll explain tomorrow. Right now I just need to go to sleep." Cass looked at Alix for a long moment. "Goodnight, Alix."

"Goodnight, Cass."

AJ was the first to wake up the next morning. He sat up, staying in bed so he could take advantage of the silence to think.

All in all, the only injuries that were really worrisome were the ones done to the emotions of the entire Heroics team. Between losing a friend and being betrayed by half of the people they knew, the day before had been a very rough one.

227

As far as physical injuries went, most of them had something going on, and a few were serious, but nothing was life threatening.

Kate's nose had indeed been broken, and it would be swollen and bruised for a while.

Justin had a severely broken hand, which would take a while to heal. It would be some time before AJ could accurately say how badly the boy's archery would be affected.

Three of Jay's ribs were fractured, and one was bruised. He couldn't stand up straight and couldn't really sit down either, and so he had been ordered to stay in bed until he could do at least one of those things, with the sole exception of attending the funeral.

Julian's shoulder was dislocated badly. He would probably have issues with moving it for years to come. He also had a deep gash down the side of his leg that had required seven stitches and had added him to the list of people who couldn't properly walk.

Kara, also on that list, had a leg that was broken in three places. She had a large cast on it, and she could only easily move around by flying. She was also covered in cuts and bruises, some from her normal fighting and some from being slammed into the building, the same incident that had broken her leg.

Ray's ankle was broken. His decision to continue fighting on it meant that it had been damaged more than it originally would have been. It was possible that he could end up with a permanent limp.

Alix was still having trouble seeing. The burn on her left hand was minor, but it had been aggravated by a gash that she had received during the fighting.

AJ, Casey, and Niall had managed to escape from the day virtually unscathed. All three of them had cuts and bruises, but they had received the lowest amount of pain and suffering.

As for Cass...

AJ looked down. Cass was still sound asleep next to him. Through the darkness, he could see the bruising around her neck and the bandage that had been put on the cut on her cheek. She had two bruised ribs in addition to the two injuries that he could see. It wasn't quite as bad as some of the injuries the kids had gotten, but he was still worried about her.

She hadn't told him what had happened between her and Wechsler. He knew that her father had been killed, and that she had something to do with it, but she had been sketchy with details.

He didn't blame her, really. She had been exhausted by the time they'd had time alone to talk, and had passed out mere seconds after getting into bed. Even though he had wanted to get more information out of her, there was no part of him that would have tried to keep her awake to do so.

AJ silently watched Cass sleep, reaching over to gently brush a stray strand of hair off of her face. It still amazed him that she, despite being injured and having just caused her father's death in some way, had still been the one taking care of him. Instead of just going to rest as soon as the mess had settled down, she insisted on accompanying him as he examined the injuries of the kids. She had stayed by his side until she wandered away to talk to Alix, but she had stayed awake until he had finally been able to go to bed himself. She kept him company, even when she should have passed out hours before she actually did so.

With a quiet sigh, AJ forced himself to get up and out of bed. He figured that he should probably prepare himself for a long day full of whining, pained teenagers, as well as the decisions that had to be made regarding the mess in the basement and first floor.

AJ got dressed quickly, electing not to wear his tie for the first time in months. It was going to be a long, tiring day, and he was certainly not going to bother looking professional for it.

He pulled on a black t-shirt and buttoned his jeans, and then headed for the door. Before he could reach for the handle, Cass's voice interrupted him.

"You know, it's cute when you fumble in the dark to get dressed, trying to be as quiet as possible so you don't wake me up."

"I don't… fumble," AJ protested quietly.

"Oh, please, you're like the world's worst football receiver."

"Don't make sports jokes. They have a tendency to go over my head."

"Mine too, which is why I'm proud of that one." Cass looked over at him. "I was going to talk to you last night, but I was too tired to."

"Talk to me about what?"

She paused. "It's nothing. Never mind."

"You brought it up."

230

"Alix said that when we were kids you and I kissed and had feelings for each other," she blurted out after a brief pause.

AJ froze. "Seriously?"

"Yeah. I guess that explains a lot. Subconsciously we were attracted to each other before we even remember meeting." He could practically hear her smile as she added, "There's something else that I wanted to talk to you about, too."

"Am I going to want to know this or...?"

"Justin told me about your fight."

AJ shifted awkwardly. "Oh?"

"Yeah, how you basically threatened him for his attitude towards me and Alix."

"Well... I know you fight your own battles, but... he just kind of pissed me off, and-"

"You don't need to defend yourself, AJ," Cass said, laughing softly so as not to put strain on her damaged ribs. Through the darkness he could see her grin. "Actually, I've seen angry AJ, and he's kind of hot. Angry AJ verbally beating up someone obnoxious because of something that was said to me? Kind of doubly hot."

He rubbed at his neck, momentarily wishing that he had decided to wear a tie so that he could fidget with it. "Yeah well... I'm glad."

"And now you're embarrassed. You're adorable. I'm starting to wish that I wasn't injured."

AJ coughed quietly. "Cass," he said in a warning tone. "Please don't come on to me in the morning when I'll need to deal with injured kids all day and can't do anything about the frustration that you cause when you torment me like this."

Cass playfully threw a pillow at him. "Then go away so that I can go back to sleep."

AJ caught the pillow with one hand and tossed it back to her. "You could've just said that in the first place," he pointed out with a laugh.

"Where would the fun be in that?"

He grinned, but kept watching her for a moment. "Hey, Cass?"

"Yes, AJ?"

"I think we're going to be okay."

She smiled. "Yeah. Yeah, I think we are." As she put her head back down, she said, "What's the plan for today?"

"Well, dealing with the kids. And figuring out what to do with the basement and the first floor. And..." He trailed off uncomfortably, and the mood instantly darkened.

"Oh," Cass whispered. "That's right. We need to plan... plan Lori's..."

AJ sighed. "Yeah. We do."

As he walked towards the kitchen, AJ saw the faint glow of a tablet coming from under the door to the library. He opened the door and stepped inside, finding Kate curled up on the sofa. "Kate? What are you doing up?"

"I couldn't sleep."

He sat down on the couch next to her feet. "I can understand why."

"I finally figured out what's been bothering me," she said quietly.

"What do you mean?"

"Something's been nagging me, something in the back of my mind that I couldn't quite put a finger on." She handed AJ her tablet. "Redhawk."

"The guy that attacked you when you were with Niall?"

"Yeah. He was supposed to still be in prison. Two year sentence, given to him one year ago." Kate blinked at AJ, the glow causing shadows on her face that made her broken nose look worse. "He disappeared from the prison system at the same time as Quake and two of the bank robbers that mysteriously had powers. I'd bet that Clarice took them. She apparently lost her mind a long time ago, and Alix said that she found some files suggesting that Alice Cage was behind the escapes, so it'd make sense."

"Well, Porter is in prison, and Alice Cage is dead. So we don't need to worry about whatever she was planning with them."

"I'm aware of that. But a few dozen other criminals have vanished from the system in the past two years. So where are they now?"

AJ shrugged. "I guess we have something to do when you kids are all fixed up again."

"You don't seem very concerned about this," Kate noted.

"I am, but honestly, Kate, I'm too tired to worry about it until we can actually do something about it."

The teenager nodded. "Fair enough."

AJ stood up, pausing to kiss Kate on the top of the head. "Try to get some sleep, kiddo. We've worried enough about problems caused by Alice Cage to last us for a good long while."

A week after the battle it was Lori's funeral, and like the movie cliché, it was raining.

The Heroics team, some of Lori's school friends, and Zach and a few other Security Legion members were all in attendance. The school kids had almost definitely figured out why Lori had died, and who the other attendees were in their free time, but they seemed to be ignoring it out of respect. The reason for the obviousness was how battered all of the heroes were. Kate's broken nose had only gotten worse visually, Julian's arm was in a sling, and Kara and Ray were both on crutches.

Zach was standing next to Casey, his hand resting on the small of her back comfortingly. She had another funeral to go to that day, for her mother, which the Heroics kids had been forbidden from so as to not draw attention to how many people they had lost. While they would never admit it, most of them hadn't even been sure if they had wanted to go anyway, given what they had learned about the woman.

Cass too had another funeral, this one the next day. She was standing next to AJ closely, paler than usual. She still hadn't told the others what exactly had happened to her father, and for the most part they doubted that she ever would.

Bobby and Johnny had also shown up, standing a good distance away from everyone. There had been mutual agreement that Clarice and Dick had manipulated their fellow Alumni members, and the two surviving subordinates shouldn't be held responsible for doing what they thought was their job. The slain Alumni had been buried the day before, and from the look of Bobby's clothes, he hadn't bothered to change. The blank look in his eyes that had appeared after his sister's death hadn't left, and Johnny looked worried as he held his hand.

When the funeral was over, the two men were the first to vanish from the cemetery, obviously not wanting to end up in a conversation with the Heroics members.

The team began to head out as well, much more slowly. Zach had lowered his hand, but he was still walking close to Casey, clearly wanting to keep her company as she went through one of the toughest days of her life. In an attempt to distract them all, he asked, "What's the plan with the damage to the mansion?"

"Well we obviously need to repair it," Cass said. "We'll probably take the time to do some reformatting. Put in some things that we might need, add some space, reorganize. That type of stuff."

"Maybe a better fire control system," Niall added lightly. He had an arm around a shivering Kate's shoulders.

"I think we should repair the whole mansion," Casey said. "The outside too. Make it known that people live there. That *we* live there."

AJ seemed surprised. "Won't that make it a bit more obvious who we are? A group of kids living under one roof who perfectly match the basic descriptions of a group of kid vigilantes?"

"Maybe. But I'm tired of hiding, AJ," Casey replied. "We hid for years because even our leader didn't want us to exist. We're fake people with fake lives, hiding in the shadows to avoid the very people we're trying to protect. We shouldn't be doing that."

"I'd be the first to agree, but it might be dangerous." Zach sounded concerned.

Casey gave a short laugh. "After these past few weeks, Zach, I don't think dangerous is something we should be worrying about. Secrets aren't going to keep the danger away. They just make the danger harder to deal with."

"I agree with Casey," Kate said, speaking for the first time that day. "I want to be able to admit that you guys are my family. I don't want to hide anymore. We're going to finish healing and then go back to what we do best, because we're fighters. And we can't stop fighting."

Alix adjusted the sunglasses that she was forced to wear even in the dim light of the rainy day. "Do you think we can pull it off?"

Kate gave a thin smile. "Of course we can, Thief. We're Heroics."

EPILOGUE

A five-year-old girl with dark hair paused on the steps of her school, frowning at the gray-haired woman who was leaning against the building. "Who are you?" the girl asked curiously. "I've never seen you before."

"I'm Ms. Shade, the new eighth grade advanced science teacher. Who are you?"

"Brooke. Brooke Hamil," the girl answered cautiously.

"Nice to meet you, Brooke." The woman smiled. "I presume that I'll be seeing you in my class soon?"

Brooke laughed. "I'm only in first grade."

"Soon enough. You seem like a smart kid. Besides, it'll get here faster than you think."

"My dad always says that. He seems to be dreading the day that I become a teenager. I think he's worried that I'm too much like my mom."

"I'm sure he doesn't mean it to be a bad thing." As the bell rang, the woman stood up straight. "Well, I suppose we both should be getting to class."

The girl nodded, flashed a quick smile, and ran into the building.

"Too much like her mother, huh? For her sake, I certainly hope not," the woman whispered as her metal-gray gaze watched the little girl go.

About The Author

Alex Kost lives in southern New Jersey under the disguise of her mild-mannered alter ego Laura Wilson. She lives with her parents and her dog while she attends The College Of New Jersey, studying Communications: Radio/TV/Film with a minor in Creative Writing. She is an on-again-off-again volunteer at her local public library and a full-time geek.

If you'd like to discuss *Harry Potter*, debate *Star Wars*, or ask any questions, you can find her at alexkost.tumblr.com.